CHAPTER ONE

"One, two, it is coming for you?"

Laura Smith was in a world of her own. The seven-year-old was blissfully unaware that she was being observed. Detective Sergeant Jason Smith was watching his daughter from the doorway of her bedroom.

"Three, four," she carried on singing. "Lock the cellar door."

Smith cringed. He wasn't quite sure if he liked the direction this seemingly harmless song was heading.

"Five, six, pray you don't get sick.

The rhyme was taking on a rather sinister tone, but Smith was curious. He carried on listening.

"Seven, eight," Laura sang. "Pray it's not too late. Nine, ten, never breathe again."

Smith had heard enough. He coughed to let Laura know he was there. She smiled at him from the bed.

"Where did you learn that?" Smith asked.

"Timothy Green taught me it," Laura said.

"The Australian kid?"

Timothy had come to Laura's school a month ago, and she'd been obsessed with the boy ever since.

"He smells funny, remember," Smith reminded her.

"He doesn't smell anymore."

"It's a terrible song anyway," Smith said.

"It is not. It rhymes."

"But there's no real flow to it. For example, the word *pray* is used in two consecutive lines. That's bad form."

"Bad what?" Laura said.

"Never mind." Smith didn't feel like explaining it to a little girl. "Where did the Green kid even come up with something like that?"

"It's all about the Chinese germs," Laura explained. "They're coming."

For once, Smith was lost for words.

He was as aware as everyone else in the country that something nasty was brewing. The virus was a hot topic – COVID-19 was on everybody's lips and the media had reported on very little else for weeks. The previous day Tedros Ghebreyesus, the director general of the World Health Organization had declared COVID-19 a pandemic and expressed concerns about the alarming levels of spread and the severity of the outbreak.

Smith knew very little about it, but he did know it was serious. Huge changes were on the cards and widespread panic was setting in. Smith had had a lot of time to dwell on it. He'd been off work for over three weeks. It wasn't by choice. He'd been told in no uncertain terms he was not to set foot inside the station until his compulsory sick leave was over. It wasn't up for debate. Smith had suffered his fair share of injuries during his career but the most recent one was by far the worst. The man the team had dubbed The Electrician had almost succeeded in ending Smith's life before Laura's Chinese germs had the chance to get hold of him.

Laura was now humming the tune. Smith left her to it. He went downstairs and made some coffee. Whitton was at work and Lucy was visiting Darren Lewis. Smith and Whitton's adopted teenage daughter was pregnant and she was already halfway there. Soon, things were going to change in the Smith household, and he wasn't looking forward to it. The father of the baby, Darren *bloody* Lewis had insisted he would be there every step of the way – he was going to take care of Lucy and the baby, but Smith still wasn't convinced that was going to happen. Darren was still a child himself.

Smith took the coffee outside and lit a cigarette. The doctors who'd treated him in hospital had tried to persuade him to quit, but Smith wasn't quite ready for that yet so he'd promised to cut down a bit, and he now limited himself to ten cigarettes per day. It was just after four in the afternoon and he'd already used up his ration for the day. He told himself he would cancel that out tomorrow. He'd promised himself the very same thing yesterday.

The sun was low in the sky but it was unseasonably warm. Spring had arrived early and stayed put. Smith sat down at the table and sighed deeply. He wasn't wired to sit at home all day and it was starting to take its toll. He'd tried to get reacquainted with his guitar but even that hadn't helped. At best he'd only managed an hour or so on his beloved Fender before he tired of it. He needed to work. He needed to get stuck into a juicy murder investigation – that was just how he was made.

Theakston and Fred came outside. The chubby Bull Terrier and the gruesome Pug were joined at the hip these days. Theakston sniffed the air and lifted his leg. Fred waited for him to finish, inspected the patch of grass Theakston had urinated on then followed suit. Both of them headed back inside the house. That was as much action as they were going to see today. Smith knew they would now make themselves comfortable on the sofa in the living room and that's where they would stay.

He finished his cigarette, and he was debating whether to light another when the ringtone of his mobile phone sounded inside. Pink Floyd's *Shine on you Crazy Diamond* had been the sound of his phone for years and Smith never tired of it. He went inside and saw from the screen that it was Whitton.

"Are you missing me?" Smith said.

"Everybody is," Whitton told him.

"It won't be long now. The appointment with the doc is tomorrow, and I'm sure I can persuade him to declare me fit for duty. What's happening at the madhouse?"

"Something nasty."

"I want in," Smith said.

"A call came in from a man in Scarcroft," Whitton said. "He owns a few properties there and he phoned about squatters in one of the houses."

"Squatters are a matter for the council," Smith reminded her.

"These ones are our problem. Uniform went to the house and found something they weren't expecting. In the cellar of the house were the partially decomposed bodies of three men."

CHAPTER TWO

Whitton parked her car outside number 12 Nunthorpe Road and got out. Bridge's Toyota was already there. He and DC Harry Moore were engaged in a conversation next to it. DI Oliver Smyth was talking on his mobile phone further down the street. The blue lights on the two police cars were flashing in the late-afternoon half-light. An ambulance was on hand even though by all accounts the men in the cellar of number 12 wouldn't need it.

Whitton walked over to Bridge and DC Moore.

"What do we know?"

"We haven't been inside," Bridge said. "Webber has just got here, and him and Billie are taking a look now."

"Word is there are three of them inside," DC Moore added. "Three men in an advanced state of decomposition. The owner of the house has had problems with squatters in the past and he'd had enough. He came in mob-handed to get them out, but he wasn't expecting what he found."

"I bet he wasn't."

"How's that husband of yours?" Bridge asked.

"Like a bear with a sore head," Whitton said. "He's unbearable when he's not working. He's got his final assessments with the doctor and the psychologist tomorrow and hopefully it'll be good news. For all our sakes. I wonder what happened to the three men."

"I'm sure we'll find out soon enough."

DI Smyth joined them. His face was still tanned from his recent trip to Thailand.

"Webber is going to be busy for some time," he said. "He's confirmed that we've got three dead males. I want a door-to-door. Somebody must know who these men are."

"Who has a cellar in their house?" DC Moore wondered.

"It's not common," DI Smyth said. "But some of the old houses have basement rooms. Webber thinks they were imprisoned down there. The door was locked with a padlock on the outside."

"Bloody hell," Bridge said. "I wonder why nobody heard them. Surely you'd make a bit of a din if someone locked you in."

"We still don't know what we're dealing with," DI Smyth said. "There are no windows down in the cellar, and it's possible the room was soundproofed. We'll know more when forensics have finished, but I want that door-to-door right now. One of the neighbours might be able to shed some light on who these men are."

"Where's the owner of the house?" Whitton asked.

"He had to check on one of his other properties."

"And you let him leave?" DC Moore said.

"I don't very much like your tone, Harry. He's the one who called it in, and he's been told his presence will be requested at the station. We've got his details, and he was very obliging. Get moving with that door-to-door."

His phone started to ring again. He walked away to take the call.

"He's in a good mood," DC Moore said.

"He's been like that since he got back from Thailand," Bridge said. "Perhaps he hooked up with a young Thai girl over there, and he misses her."

"Let's get moving." Whitton said. "Harry, those two are standing around twiddling their thumbs. Put them to work. We need to speak to all of the people in the neighbouring houses."

She was talking about the two uniformed officers standing next to one of the police cars. It was PC Black and PC Miller.

"Will do, Sarge," DC Moore said.

"We might as well make ourselves useful," Bridge said. "Don't look now but we have a curtain twitcher at six o' clock. Nosy neighbours are always a good thing at times like these."

The curtain twitcher turned out to be a woman by the name of Maggie Pratt. She lived at number 10 – next door to the house where the three men had perished. She answered the door almost as soon as Bridge had pressed the bell. She invited them in and offered them something to drink. Whitton declined.

"What's going on?" Maggie asked. "What's with all the police? Is someone dead?"

The face mask she was wearing was too big for her face, and it had slipped down past her nose. She pulled it up, but it just slipped down again.

"What makes you ask that?" Bridge said.

"What other explanation could there be? You lot don't come out in force for a house burglary. I'm right aren't I?"

"We don't know what happened yet," Whitton said. "Have you lived here long?"

"Over thirty years."

"Do you know your neighbour?" Bridge said. "The man at number 12?"

"He's not my neighbour. He doesn't live there."

"Who lives there?" Whitton said.

"They come and go. And I can tell you some of them are not exactly savoury. This used to be a nice place to live. That was until people like Miller started exploiting the system."

"I'm not following you," Bridge said.

"Housing benefit. It's guaranteed rent, isn't it? No need to chase the tenants for the money. Problem is, people like Miller don't give a hoot what sort they let into their houses."

"Is Mr Miller the owner of number 12?" Whitton asked.

"That's right. I saw him lingering earlier. What's he done? Hopefully something that'll put him away for a good few years."

"As far as we're aware," Bridge said. "Mr Miller hasn't done anything. Do you know if there was anyone living at number 12 recently?"

"I don't like to pry," Maggie said.

"Right," Bridge said. "But you must have noticed people coming and going – living next door, I mean."

A large white cat came in and stretched its legs. It hopped up onto a single-seater chair and stared right at Bridge. Its gaze was unnerving, and Bridge had to look away.

"Did you see anybody coming in and out of number 12?" Whitton asked Maggie.

"Not for a while," she said.

"When was the last time you saw someone next door?" Bridge said.

"Probably about a week ago."

"Mr Miller called us about squatters," Whitton said. "Did you happen to notice them?"

"How would I know? What does a squatter even look like?"

Whitton didn't have an answer to that.

"The people you remembered seeing," she said. "Were they men or women?"

"Both," Maggie said. "I think. Like I said, I don't like to pry."

"Were they young or old?" Bridge said.

"Mostly young. About your age."

Bridge was due to celebrate his thirtieth birthday in a couple of months.

"Do you recall any disturbances next door?" Whitton said. "Any raised voices? Heated arguments?"

"All the time," Maggie said. "They were an unsavoury bunch."

"And you haven't seen anybody next door for a week?" Bridge said.

"Not that I remember. It's been quiet since just after St David's Day. I'm Welsh, you know."

Whitton didn't think they were going to get anything useful from Maggie Pratt. She indicated this to Bridge by getting to her feet. Bridge stood up too.

"Thank you for your time," Whitton said. "If you think of anything else, please give me a call."

She took out one of her cards and handed it to her.

"If one of those undesirables is dead," Maggie said. "If that's the reason the place is swarming with police, good riddance to them."

"Thank you for your time," Whitton said once more.

The cat hissed at them as they left the room.

CHAPTER THREE

"She was a prime example of an upstanding citizen," Bridge said outside.

"It's the way of the world," Whitton said. "People are getting more and more opposed to change. It's the English way. We don't like it when things aren't like they were thirty years ago."

"Since when did you become a pensioner?"

"Shut up. It looks like Webber is finished."

She nodded down the street. The Head of Forensics was putting something into the boot of his car. Billie Jones, his assistant was standing next to him.

"Just look at that arse," Bridge said. "I have to pinch myself every morning. To think a specimen like that chose me."

"It is hard to believe," Whitton agreed. "You two are getting serious, aren't you?"

"We are," Bridge confirmed. "Billie Jones is the one."

Whitton sighed. "I want to know what's in that cellar."

She walked up to Webber. It was hard to gauge from the expression on his face how bad it was down in the cellar. He rarely expressed emotion at the scene of a crime.

"Afternoon," Whitton said. "What are we looking at?"

"Three dead males," Webber said. "Judging by the state of decomposition I'd say they've been down there for at least a week."

"Are you finished in there?"

"Far from it," Webber said. "We're going to be down there for most of the day. I just needed some fresh air. It's not just the cellar itself we need to go over – there's another room down there."

"What's in there?" Whitton asked.

"We don't know yet. There's a reinforced steel door and it's locked. We're going to need specialist equipment to open it."

"What about the three men, Whitton said. "Any sign of injuries?"

"None that I could see. But we'll know for certain after the postmortems. If I were to hazard a guess, I'd say they died from severe dehydration. There's no running water in the cellar and we couldn't find any sign of food or bottled water."

"Do you think they were imprisoned down there?" Whitton asked.

"There was a padlock on the outside of the cellar door," Webber said. "And we found a lot of scratch marks on the inside of the door. Dr Bean will probably find evidence to show these men tried to get through that door."

"Why didn't anybody hear them?" Whitton wondered. "If somebody locked me up in a cellar, I would make a hell of a din."

"You could hold a rave in that cellar and the neighbours would be none the wiser. The walls are not only triple insulated – they've been soundproofed too. Looks like a pro job."

Whitton was finding this hard to digest. Why would someone go to all this trouble? Why would someone want to imprison three men in a cellar?

"I don't suppose you found anything to help us ID the men," she said.

"Nothing," Webber told her. "Someone wanted these men to die in the most horrible way and they wanted their identifications to remain a mystery."

"Can I take a look?"

"It's not pretty down there."

"It never is," Whitton said.

Webber nodded. "You know the drill. How's Smith bearing up? Don't tell him I said this but I miss the Australian pain in the arse."

"Your secret's safe with me," Whitton assured him. "Hopefully he'll be back at work in a few days. He's got an assessment tomorrow to see if he's physically and mentally fit to return to active duty."

"Smith has never been mentally fit for anything," Webber said. "And you can tell him I said that."

"I'll make sure I do. Have you got a SOC suit for me?"

Whitton stopped in the doorway of number 12 and took a number of deep breaths in quick succession. She went inside and the smell hit her straight away. It was the smell of murder – the stench of death rarely changed. The thick putrid funk crept inside the nose and mouth and refused to budge. It stayed for hours afterwards, and it could be detected on the clothes and in the hair for a very long time.

Whitton took in the house. Number 12 Nunthorpe Road was a typical Victorian three-storey property. Recently many of these houses had been converted into student accommodation. A savvy landlord could stick five or six students in one single property. Whitton wondered why this house was standing empty. Maggie Pratt had mentioned something about the landlord renting it out to people on benefits, but the more Whitton looked around the more she realised this house hadn't been occupied for quite some time.

A PC Whitton didn't recognise was standing outside the door to the cellar, preventing anyone from going down there. Whitton nodded to him and made her way down the stairs. The stench was much worse down here, but Whitton expected it to be. If the three men had been dead for at least a week nature had had plenty of time to get to work on them. And the lack of windows in the cellar didn't help matters.

The room was lit only by the two powerful spotlights Webber had set up which led Whitton to believe there were no lights down here. The thought made her feel sick. These men had been shut in with no food or water – with no hope of escape and they'd been left in utter darkness.

The human body can keep going for a couple of weeks without food, but water is a different kettle of fish altogether. The effects of dehydration happen quickly. Whitton gauged the ambient temperature inside the cellar to be around thirty degrees and that won't have helped. After the first day the men will have been incapable of perspiring. Their body temperatures would rise and this would result in a severe drop in blood pressure. The men wouldn't be able to urinate, and this would cause toxin levels to build. The kidneys would then be forced to work at triple their normal speed and they would eventually fail. After three days without water there would be widespread organ failure and certain death. It really was a terrible way to die.

The first thing that struck Whitton was the positioning of the bodies. All three men were laid, side by side on the floor at the bottom of the stairs. Whitton didn't know what that meant. Was it possible they'd been placed like that after they died? If that was the case pathology would confirm it.

The skin on the faces of all three men was very similar. Their eyes were sunken, and the skin was a sickly yellow colour. The lips of two of the men had cracked open revealing the teeth underneath. It was impossible to determine the age of the men. They'd aged drastically in the time they'd spent down in the cellar.

The door Webber had spoken about was located next to the staircase. Whitton rapped her fingers on it and it was clear it was very thick – at least three inches. Whitton wondered what lay beyond it. Why fit such a door in the cellar of a house? Someone really didn't want anybody to get inside the room it was blocking off.

There wasn't much more to see. Whitton determined that all three men had been imprisoned in the cellar for quite some time and all three had died of what could possibly be termed natural causes. Nevertheless, the circumstances surrounding the deaths were suspicious and Whitton was left in no doubt that this would be the beginning of another murder investigation.

CHAPTER FOUR

Smith was lost in a song he hadn't played in years. It had taken him some time to get the tone on the amplifier just right, but he'd persevered and with a bit of tweaking he'd managed to recreate the perfect sound to do justice to *Django* by Joe Bonamassa. He'd turned up the volume much louder than he usually did but the song necessitated it. The track was one of his favourites – it was a simple guitar-only song without lyrics, but the music told its own story.

Three minutes in and Smith was getting ready to savour the crescendo when he was stopped by an ungodly scream. His fingers flew down the fretboard and the resulting screech made him cringe. Laura was standing in the doorway with Smith's phone in her hand.

"Why did you scream?" he asked her.

"Because you weren't listening."

Smith couldn't argue with the logic behind this.

"Your phone has been ringing for ages," Laura said and handed it to him.

"Do you have to play so loud?"

"It wasn't that loud," Smith argued.

Laura gave him a look only a seven-year-old can get away with and left him with his phone. The feedback from the amplifier was getting louder so Smith switched it off. His phone started to ring again.

It was Whitton. "Where are you?"

"At home," Smith said. "Where else would I be?"

"The DI needs you to come and take a look at something."

"I'm still on sick leave," Smith reminded her.

"He'll clear it with the powers that be. Is Lucy there?"

"She's still at Darren *bloody* Lewis's house."

"Maybe you can drop Laura off at my parents' place," Whitton suggested.

"Or Shelia would be even better."

Sheila Rogers was their next-door-neighbour. Smith still wasn't sure what to make of the peculiar woman but Laura and her daughter, Fran had become close friends.

"I thought you didn't like her," Smith said. "What with that business in her back garden."

"She's apologised for that," Whitton said. "She made a mistake. I'm sure she won't mind having Laura for a few hours. The DI wants you in Scarcroft. My parents' house is on the opposite side of the city."

"I'll see what the psychotic neighbour says," Smith said. "What's in Scarcroft?"

"That's what DI Smyth needs you to tell him."

She gave him the address.

"I'll arrange something for Laura," Smith said. "I'm intrigued."

* * *

He was more than intrigued – he felt invigorated. Whitton had been rather vague, but her tone had suggested something nasty was waiting for him at number 12 Nunthorpe Road. The thought thrilled him. He'd been out of action for three weeks but as he drove through the city he sensed that was about to change. If the boss had stuck his neck out and requested Smith's presence while he was still technically on sick leave it could only mean one thing – it was the beginning of another murder investigation and he'd been invited to be part of the action.

It was a ten-minute drive to Scarcroft but Smith made it in five. More than one speed camera had caught him exceeding the speed limit but Smith didn't care. He would worry about that later. He parked his car behind Webber's, got out and surveyed the road. All of the houses on Nunthorpe Road were similar in build. The three-storey Victorian properties had borne witness to three different centuries. These houses had seen things they would never be able to speak of. Smith made his way to number 12 to see what this house could tell him.

He was intercepted at the front door by Grant Webber. The Head of Forensics held out his hand and this surprised Smith. He shook the hand, nevertheless.

"I never thought I'd say this," Webber said. "But it's good to have you back."

"What have we got?" Smith asked.

"You need to see for yourself. Suit up and follow me."

He led Smith down the hallway and stopped at the top of a flight of stairs. Smith's nose caught the whiff of something bad and he looked at Webber.

"The stink is worse down there," Webber pointed down the staircase.

"I'm not a big fan of cellars," Smith told him.

The *Dogwalker* investigation was still fresh in his head.

"With very good reason," Webber said. "But you'll be quite safe down there. Billie is busy photographing the room within a room."

"Room within a room?"

"I'll show you. You might want to cover your nose."

Smith placed a foot onto the first step and stopped.

"Is this going to take long?" Webber said.

Smith took a deep breath and carried on down the stairs. The first thing he registered was the temperature increased the further he descended. He stopped at the bottom and wiped his brow. The heat was stifling down here, and the stench was oppressive. Two powerful spotlights were illuminating the entire room.

Smith's eyes fell on the three dead men. They would be taken away shortly. Billie Jones appeared from a room off to the side.

"What are your thoughts on the cause of death?" Smith asked her.

"Probably dehydration," she said. "They've been here for about a week and there's no running water down here."

"And nobody heard anything? Why didn't they cry out?"

"They probably did," Billie said. "But the entire room has been soundproofed. It looks like a pro job."

"What could anybody possibly gain from this?" Smith wondered. "What did they hope to achieve by locking three men in a cellar with no food or water?"

"Four."

Webber looked Smith right in the eye.

"There's another one in there." He pointed to the gap that used to be filled with the thick metal door.

The door was now propped up against one of the walls. It had taken over an hour with a blowtorch to gain access to the hidden room.

Smith walked towards it. He gasped when he realised what was contained within. It looked like some kind of hospital room. Against one of the walls was a bed not dissimilar to the ones found in hospital wards. There was a figure on the bed and it wasn't moving.

There was a table next to the bed with an empty glass and a blister packet of pills on it. On the opposite wall was a filing cabinet and a small bookcase. Smith took a closer look and that's when he spotted what appeared to be some kind of journal.

"Have you finished in here?" he asked Webber.

"I wouldn't have brought you down here if we hadn't," Webber said. "What's on your mind?"

Smith picked up the journal and showed it to him. "The date on the front is the first of this month. That's almost two weeks ago."

"And it makes for confusing reading," Billie told him. "I just had a quick look, but it's written in a language I've never seen before."

"It's yours when we've gone over it," Webber said.

"What happened here?" Smith asked nobody in particular. "I can't make any sense of this scene. Three dead men in the cellar and another corpse in the room attached to it. What the hell happened to them?"

The question went unanswered when a sound from the bed caused all three of them to look in that direction.

The man coughed again and opened his eyes. Webber had been mistaken in his body count. The man on the bed was still alive.

CHAPTER FIVE

"How could he have made a mistake like that?"

Smith and Whitton had just finished eating and Smith had offered to wash the dishes. Laura and Lucy had excused themselves and headed up to their respective rooms.

"How could he not know the bloke was still alive?" he added.

"Mistakes happen," Whitton said.

"But Grant Webber is rarely the one who makes them. He's going to get into shit for this – it should have been the first thing he checked."

Whitton rubbed her eyes. "The investigation has barely started and already it's being run as though a wet-behind-the-ears detective is in charge."

Smith scrubbed at some stubborn grease on a plate. "What do you mean by that?"

"The DI shouldn't have let you anywhere near a crime scene when you were still on sick leave."

"You told me it was all above board."

"It was," Whitton said. "Until Webber made his rookie error. The man in the other room was in a bad way. If he doesn't make it there will be a full enquiry. If it transpires that Webber's lapse was responsible for the man's death they're going to scrutinise every aspect of what went on in that cellar today, and that includes your presence there. People could lose their jobs over this."

Smith placed the dishcloth on the peg on the wall and pulled the plug to drain the water from the sink.

"Do you want a beer?" Whitton asked him.

"No thanks," Smith replied.

"Are you feeling alright?"

"Never better," Smith said. "But if I'm to stand a chance of persuading a shrink to let me get back to work I don't want to go in there tomorrow stinking of beer. I don't think it would help my case."

"What did you make of that cellar?" Whitton asked.

"Something happened down there that doesn't bear thinking about – something horrific. What do we know about the owner of the property?"

"Arthur Miller," Whitton said. "He owns a few houses in that area. We spoke to the neighbour, and she told us the tenants come and go. It's mostly people on housing benefit. Do you think he could be involved?"

"I don't know enough about him, but he should be our prime suspect right now."

"The DI doesn't seem to think so."

"What is it with the boss?" Smith asked. "Why isn't this Miller guy being interrogated as we speak?"

"DI Smyth has been acting weird ever since he came back from Thailand," Whitton said. "I'm wondering if something happened while he was over there. His mind hasn't been on the job."

"I'll have a word with him," Smith said. "Find out what's going on."

"He won't thank you for it."

"Since when has that bothered me? I'm going out for a smoke."

"How many have you had today?"

"Not many," Smith lied.

He went outside and the dogs followed him. Theakston and Fred ran to the bottom of the garden and lifted their legs in unison. Smith found it highly amusing, and he wondered if they'd rehearsed this at some stage. He considered going to fetch his phone to record their bizarre, synchronized pissing but reckoned the moment would be gone by the time he got back out. He lit a cigarette and closed his eyes. A smile formed on his face, and he let it grow. He was back – he could feel it. The three weeks he'd been off work felt like ten times that and he'd missed it.

The scene in the cellar in Scarcroft was a strange one and Smith couldn't understand it. Three men had perished from what they believed to be dehydration and another man was in a critical condition at the hospital. Logic dictated that he was their main priority and Smith hoped and prayed that he would pull through from his ordeal. He was the key to finding out what happened to the other men.

Smith's thoughts turned to Webber and DI Smyth. Both of them were experienced officers and both were extremely competent in their jobs, but The Head of Forensics and the DI had made huge blunders today. Smith couldn't figure that out either. He'd lost count of how many murders Webber had worked on – he was always first on the scene and he was the most meticulous man Smith had ever encountered. How did he not realise the man in the secret room was still alive?

And why had DI Smyth dismissed the owner of the property as a suspect so quickly? That made absolutely no sense whatsoever. If Smith was in charge of the investigation Arthur Miller would be hauled in and held in custody for as long as was permitted according to the law. He would know that house inside out – he'll be able to tell them why the cellar has a secret room hidden by a heavy-duty door, so why was he not in custody?

Smith went back inside the house and heard Whitton's voice in the living room. She was talking to someone on the phone. Smith turned on the kettle and caught the end of her conversation.

Thank you for letting me know.

She came into the kitchen and Smith knew something was wrong. He'd learned how to read his wife over the years.

"Bad news?"

"The worst," Whitton said. "The man found in the secret room didn't make it. I've just spoken to DC King at the hospital. According to the medical staff it was a miracle he lasted as long as he did. Heads are going to roll for this."

"We don't know that," Smith said. "If the docs said he shouldn't have survived that long it probably wouldn't have made a difference whether Webber cottoned on that he was still alive when they went in."

"Come on, Jason," Whitton said. "You know how it goes. It should have been the first thing he checked. You're first on scene you make damn sure about something like that. There is a shitstorm heading our way."

Smith was glad when his own phone started to ring. The ringtone told him it was DI Smyth. During one of his many stints in hospital he'd decided to personalise all his contact's ringtones and the intro to Elvis Costello's *Oliver's Army* told him it was DI Smyth.

"It's the boss," Smith told Whitton.

"He's probably heard the bad news," she said.

He had. But as Smith listened further to what the DI had to say he knew there was something else on his mind. He suggested meeting up for a few pints in the Hog's Head and Smith had no choice but to agree. He wasn't planning on drinking tonight, but it was clear DI Smyth needed to talk and Smith couldn't refuse. He'd come to like his boss and he was also intrigued. He arranged to meet him at the pub in half an hour.

CHAPTER SIX

DI Smyth was already there when Smith arrived. He'd chosen a table far away from the bar even though the pub was quiet. It was Thursday evening and only a few of the tables were occupied. The only person sitting at the bar was an elderly man with a newspaper in front of him. Smith recognised him and he knew Marge, the owner of the Hog's Head wasn't going to get rich from him. The old man in the flat cap could nurse half a pint for hours.

Smith joined DI Smyth at the table. There were two full pints of Theakston on it.

DI Smyth nodded to them. "I took the liberty."

Smith looked at the beer, picked it up and took a long sip. "Thanks. I wasn't going to drink tonight. I didn't want to see the shrink stinking of beer. It's not a very good impression to make."

"I think he'd be more suspicious if you didn't smell of beer," DI Smyth said. "I assume you've heard."

"Whitton got a call from Kerry at the hospital. It might not be as bad as we think. The bloke was on death's door when Webber finally managed to get into that room. The docs were surprised he lasted that long. What's going on, boss?"

"I'm in a bit of a pickle," DI Smyth told him.

"Can I ask you something," Smith said.

"Of course."

"Why didn't you bring the owner of the house in for questioning? He should be in custody."

"Mr Miller isn't going anywhere, Smith," DI Smyth said. "We'll speak to him tomorrow."

Smith spotted Marge and gave her a wave. She was cleaning tables and her eyes lit up when she saw him. She walked over to their table.

"Jason. I haven't seen you for weeks."

"Doctor's orders, Marge," Smith said.

"Nothing serious I hope."

"I've had worse. How are things? It's quiet tonight."

"I never thought I'd ever say this, but sometimes I prefer it like that. Spring is on the way and it'll be all hands on deck for months. I'm thinking of getting a manager in to take some of the pressure off."

"Good idea. You know DI Smyth, don't you?"

"I never forget a face," Marge said. "Can I get you gentlemen a couple more pints?"

Smith downed what was left in his glass. "Thanks Marge."

"Talk to me," Smith said when the drinks had been replenished.

"It's a rather long story," DI Smyth said.

"It usually is. The night's still young. Are you worried about the inevitable enquiry into the death of that bloke in the cellar?"

DI Smyth sighed and took a long drink of beer. "That's the least of my worries."

"What's going on, boss?" Smith asked.

DI Smyth looked at his colleague. Smith had never seen him looking so dejected. The man Smith knew as someone who never let anything faze him looked like somebody else. His eyes were bloodshot and the bags underneath them suggested he hadn't had a good night's sleep in a very long time.

"I can trust you, can't I?" DI Smyth said.

"Do you even have to ask me that?" Smith said.

"I apologise. I'm not thinking straight right now. Haven't been since I returned from Thailand."

"What happened over there?"

"It was wonderful," DI Smyth said. "It really was. In fact, it was just what the doctor ordered. I needed the break and Thailand was everything it cracked up to be. Warm, sunny weather and beaches like you've never seen before. The food was the best I've ever tasted and the locals are the friendliest in the world. It was a dream holiday."

Smith wondered when he was going to get to the point. Where was this heading? He decided to humour his boss and let him carry on. He'd been in enough interview situations to know that sometimes it was better to just listen. Often that's when the truth was revealed.

"It was a dream holiday," DI Smyth repeated. "Up to a point. I was feeling more relaxed than I had in years. I needed the break. I needed a break from the job and I needed to get away from the God-awful English weather and I was actually dreading coming home. At one stage I even debated whether to throw caution to the wind for once in my life and stay put."

"You were thinking about not coming home?" Smith said.

"It did cross my mind, but you know what it's like on holiday. It's just that – a holiday, and it would have been foolhardy to throw away everything I had back home on a whim. Will you excuse me? I need to use the Gents."

Smith looked at his watch. Only five minutes had elapsed since DI Smyth had started telling his rather long-winded tale, but it felt like much more time had passed. Smith wasn't a big fan of beating about the bush and he decided he would push the DI to get to the point when he came back. His phone started to ring, and he ignored it when he saw from the screen it was his next-door neighbour. Sheila Rogers was the last person he felt like talking to. What he really felt like was leaving the Hog's Head and going straight home.

DI Smyth returned with two more pints of Theakston. Smith drained half of his in one go. He needed it.

"Where was I?" DI Smyth asked.

"You were about to tell me what happened in Thailand that has got you in the state you're in now?" Smith decided to come out with it. "I've never seen you like this before. Whitton has noticed it too. She said you haven't been the same since you came back from holiday."

DI Smyth looked around the room. If Smith didn't know any better, he would swear he was making sure they weren't being overheard.

"I'm in big trouble."

"What kind of trouble?" Smith asked.

"I met someone while I was over there."

"But that's great."

"So I thought, but things aren't always what they seem to be. I thought we were happy together. I know what you must be thinking – holiday romances and all that, but this felt like the real deal. Until I got a glimpse of the other side of the person I met."

"What happened?" Smith said.

"We parted ways. I was the one to break it off and it wasn't appreciated. Two days after I got back, I received an email with some attachments that could make life very difficult for me. The person I met in Thailand is threatening blackmail."

"Blackmail?" Smith wasn't expecting this. "What are they planning on blackmailing you with?"

DI Smyth took out his phone and opened up his emails. He clicked on the one he wanted and opened the attachment. He sighed deeply. Whatever he was looking at was clearly causing him a lot of pain.

"This is what I was sent," he said. "There's more of them, and he's threatening to show these to everybody I know. My family, friends and work colleagues - everybody."

He handed Smith the phone and at first the Australian detective wasn't sure what he was looking at. Then it dawned on him.

"Ah," he said.

CHAPTER SEVEN

"Spare some change?"

Marcus Green had been plying his trade in the area around the Minster for three years. His was a strange tale and it was a story he would tell to anyone who was willing to part with some coins for the privilege. Marcus had been living on the streets for over a decade and his story was different to many of the homeless souls around the country in that he chose to follow this way of life voluntarily.

The son of a lawyer and an accountant, Marcus grew up oblivious to the plight of the thousands of men and woman forced to eke out an existence on the streets. A chance meeting with a homeless man in Bristol changed everything for him. Marcus quit his medical degree in the final year and walked away from college with the clothes on his back and fifteen pounds in his pocket. He didn't tell anyone about his sudden lifestyle change and his parents stopped looking for him after only a year had passed.

Marcus hitchhiked from Bristol to Newcastle but he found there was too much competition in the begging game there so he travelled around the north and finally settled in York. This was a tourist city and tourists tended to have more to offer in the form of altruism. Marcus's current abode was on the corner of Chapter House Street, a stone's throw away from the cathedral and the brewery. Business was good here, especially after the brewery tours the tourists flocked to in their droves.

The man and woman looking down at him now didn't look like tourists and Marcus wondered if he shouldn't just cut his losses and send them on their way with a *have a nice day*, and a *God bless you*, but there was something in the eyes of the woman that told him it was worth a try. Her gaze was a curious one. She wasn't displaying the usual pity Marcus was used to – there was something else in those eyes, and Marcus couldn't quite read it.

"Is this where you live?" It was the man.

His eyes were devoid of expression, and the face mask he was wearing put Marcus in mind of a medical surgeon. The blue mask covered the man's mouth and nose and it muffled the sound of his voice. Marcus could just make out the hairs of a grey beard behind it.

"Welcome to my humble abode," Marcus offered them his standard response to the question. "Fresh air and a million-pound view."

"You sleep here?" the woman asked.

"Sleep," Marcus said. "Eat, work. Is there something I can do for you?"

"Why aren't you registered with one of the shelters?" the man asked.

Marcus was suddenly on high alert.

"Are you from social services?"

The woman started to laugh. It was a very warm laugh.

"Goodness, no," she said. "You'll have to excuse my husband. He's terribly blunt."

She opened up her handbag and took out a purse. She extracted a wad of notes and Marcus gasped. He knew enough about money to calculate there was over three hundred pounds there. The woman fanned the money and cast a glance at the man. He shrugged his shoulders and nodded. Then the woman handed the whole lot to Marcus.

"Whoa," he said. "What's going on?"

"Charity, my dear," the woman said. "Take it if you want it."

Marcus wanted it. He really wanted it. It would make life much more comfortable for quite some time. He grabbed hold of the banknotes – the woman held on to them, and for a moment Marcus wondered if this was some kind of sick joke.

It wasn't. The woman relinquished the money and smiled at the homeless man sitting cross legged on the corner of the street.

"Thank you,' Marcus said. "You don't know what this means."

"I think I do, dear," the woman said. "Use it wisely. Very soon money will be worth little more than the paper it's printed on. Dark days are coming and those who are unprepared will suffer. Are you prepared, mister homeless man?"

"I take it as it comes."

Another smile.

"Perhaps we'll meet again, young man," the woman said. "Stay safe."

Marcus watched them go. It had been a strange encounter but the comforting bulge of the wad of money in his pocket made him forget about it in an instant. Instead, he was compiling a mental shopping list. Perhaps he would treat himself to a few pints at the pub on College Street too. He hadn't been in there for a very long time.

* * *

"So, you can understand my predicament."

DI Smyth was halfway through his fourth pint. Smith still held onto the phone.

"Where was this taken?" he asked.

"In a hotel room. Without my consent. I didn't even know the camera was rolling. There are more of them but this is probably the least explicit one. What am I going to do?"

Smith handed the phone back to him. "Nail the bastard."

"He has threatened to make sure people see these photos, Smith. This could make my life very unpleasant."

"Let him. The thing with blackmailers is you take away their bargaining chips and they've got nothing left. Come on, boss, this is not that bad."

"Aren't you even shocked?"

"A little bit," Smith admitted. "But when you said you'd been blackmailed with some photos taken in Thailand this was the last thing that crossed my mind. It's not like you were caught with your pants down with some ladyboy or, even worse – a child. We all know what goes on over there. This is nothing to stress about."

"It's evidence of me spending the night with another man," DI Smyth came out with it.

"What of it?"

"It..." DI Smyth began, but that was all he managed.

"Those photos are not blackmail material, boss," Smith said. "Who took them?"

"The man I was in the embrace with. I should have known he was too good to be true."

"How did you even meet him?"

DI Smyth started to laugh and it took Smith by surprise.

"Did I say something funny?"

"You seem to be taking all this with a pinch of salt," DI Smyth said.

"How else am I supposed to take it? Smith asked. "You're a grown man – you're a good bloke and an even better boss, and I couldn't give a fuck which team you choose to bat for."

"Eloquently put but thank you."

"So, how did you meet him?" Smith said. "Where did you hook up with your blackmailer?"

"We got chatting one night in the hotel bar and we hit it off," DI Smyth said. "Or at least I thought we did. In hindsight it's clear I was being played the whole time. The man is a good ten years younger than me."

"It's probably not the first time he's pulled this scam," Smith put forward. "He gets the attention of a tourist, persuades him to go back to his room and takes some pictures with a hidden camera. They swap details and when the tourist gets home there's a surprise waiting for him. He doesn't want anyone to know what he got up to in Thailand, so he pays up. What exactly does this prick want from you?"

"Fifty grand."

Smith whistled. "That's a very lucrative business model, but his days are numbered. We're going to nail the bastard."

"And then everybody will know my secret."

"Nobody will give a fuck, boss," Smith assured him. "Things have changed – we're not living in the dark ages anymore."

"Things may have changed," DI Smyth said. "But there are still certain occupations where this kind of thing is frowned upon. The Police is one of them. It's just how it is. I need another drink."

So did Smith. He didn't expect the meeting with DI Smyth to take this particular turn. He couldn't have predicted it in a million years. He was surprised the DI was so concerned about his homosexuality coming to the attention of the people in his life. Smith knew for a fact that nobody on the team would have a problem with it. Smith certainly didn't.

"I suppose there are some questions you want to ask me," DI Smyth said when he returned to the table.

"Just one," Smith said. "How do I get hold of the bastard who thinks he can get away with blackmailing my boss?"

"I don't know where he lives."

"But he sent those photos from somewhere," Smith said. "We can trace it back. And there's the fifty grand too. How was he expecting to get paid?"

"He'll provide me with bank details. It's not like in a movie where I have to dump a bag full of cash in a trash can in the dead of night."

"Then we'll get him that way. Another thing with blackmailers is you never know when it's going to end. If you give in to him now, who's to say he won't keep coming back for more?"

DI Smyth rubbed his eyes. He really did look tired.

"Are you sure you're OK with all this? My being gay I mean."

"It doesn't change a thing, boss," Smith told him. "As long as you don't try anything with me."

DI Smyth laughed. "No chance – you're not my type."

"Glad to hear it," Smith said and downed the rest of his pint. "I'd better be off. I need to be sharp tomorrow."

"Good night," DI Smyth said. "And thank you. You don't know how relieved I am to be able to get this off my chest."

"No worries," Smith said. "I'll see you at work – hopefully very soon."

CHAPTER EIGHT

When Smith looked around the waiting room he wondered if he'd come to the right place. He'd been given the all-clear from the doctor at the hospital – physically he was in good shape for a man of his age, but there was still one hurdle to get over before he could return to work, and the appointment with Dr Fiona Vennell was in ten minutes.

He walked up to the reception desk.

"I've got an appointment with Dr Vennell."

"Jason Smith?" the young man asked.

Smith was in the right place.

"That's right," he said. "Is it always so quiet here?"

The badge on his shirt told Smith his name was Gary.

"Only on this particular day," Gary said.

"What's special about today?"

"Some people are acutely phobic about Friday the thirteenth. It's rather ironic when you think about it."

Smith couldn't see any irony in it. He told Gary as much.

"When people with Paraskevidekatriaphobia – that's the official term for it, point blank refuse to schedule an appointment here on Friday the thirteenth it's ironic. It's ironic because this is precisely the place they ought to be if they want to face that fear head on. It's a funny old world, isn't it? But I can see you don't suffer from that particular phobia."

"I don't suffer from any phobias," Smith told him.

"That's actually nothing to brag about," Gary said. "It's perfectly natural for us as a species to be afraid. It's primeval and it is also essential for the survival of the species. There have been case studies carried out that conclude that once those ancient fears are eradicated the future of homo sapiens is in very dire straits."

"Gary," a woman's voice was heard behind Smith. "Could you please leave DS Smith alone. I'm ready for him."

Smith turned to face her, and he wasn't expecting what he saw. Dr Vennell didn't look much older than Lucy. She had a very pretty face and her skin was flawless. Her brown eyes were bright and the smile she gave Smith was a genuine one. She certainly didn't look old enough to be a mental health professional.

"Please come with me," she said.

Smith followed her down a corridor. She opened a door and told Smith to take a seat.

"I apologise for Gary," she said. "He's very keen but often he tends to talk too much."

"He was a bit intense for my liking," Smith said.

Dr Vennell sat down behind a desk. Smith sat opposite her.

"Can I ask you something?" he said.

"Twenty-nine," Dr Vennell said.

"A shrink and a mind-reader to boot."

"I've been cursed with youth," Dr Vennell said. "I still get asked for ID in bars. I assure you I am qualified."

"I didn't mean anything by it," Smith said.

"I graduated from university here in York when I was twenty-two. Stayed on to complete my masters, then headed up to Edinburgh to do my PHD. I'm the real deal, Detective."

"What do you want to know about me?" Smith asked. "I'm fit for duty."

"Let's see." Dr Vennell opened up a thick file. "It says here you were dead for a minute and a half."

"Ninety-six seconds," Smith corrected. "I missed out on the record by just a few seconds."

"Interesting," Dr Vennell wrote something down on the notepad in front of her.

"I've just come from the hospital," Smith told her. "And I was given the all clear to return to active duty. I just need you to tell the powers that be the same thing."

"I see. You're keen to go back to work?"

"It's all I know," Smith said. "It's what I'm wired to do."

"You've had a colourful career. According to the records you've stood on the precipice facing death a total of eleven times. Is that a fair calculation, would you think?"

"I've lost count," Smith said. "But it sounds about right. I've been lucky."

Dr Vennell leafed through the file.

"How have you been sleeping?" she said.

"Well," Smith replied. "I haven't had a nightmare for weeks."

"Is this unusual?"

Smith debated whether to tell her about the horrific nightmares and double awakenings but he opted for the truth. He sensed this woman with the youthful face would see through any lies anyway.

"I was plagued with bad dreams for a while," he said. "Lucid dreams and double awakenings."

"Interesting," Dr Vennell said. "When did these dreams start?"

"A good few years ago. I think the first ones happened when I'd taken some time off. I needed a break and I started to have these horrendous dreams almost every night."

"That's not unusual. Your mind was processing your inner demons because it was allowed time to do so. The nightmares were an essential part of this process."

"They didn't affect how I did my job," Smith said. "I think I got used to them. I'm fit to go back to work."

Dr Vennell didn't comment on this.

"Do you often relive old cases in your mind?" she asked instead.

"All the time," Smith said. "It's impossible to forget some of them."

"Do you make time to switch off? It's very important to draw a line between work and home. Is there such a thing in your life?"

"Not really," Smith admitted. "Beer helps."

"I must admit," Dr Vennell said. "You've been very frank with me."

"I figured you'd know if I was lying."

"Probably."

"And I'm a hopeless liar," Smith added. "I find it exhausting. Are you going to put in a good word for me?"

Dr Vennell smiled at him again and Smith realised he liked her smile.

"I would very much like to see you again," she said.

"Are you telling me you're not going to let me go back to work," Smith asked.

"I'm telling you no such thing. From what I've seen you're ready for active duty."

"Why do I need to come back? If I'm ready to return to work, why do I still need your help?"

"I'm asking for *your* help, DS Smith," Dr Vennell said. "I'm doing some research for a thesis on serial killers. It's a subject that has always fascinated me. What drives people to kill? It goes against the very nature of the human species."

"You sound just like Gary now," Smith dared.

"I believe your experience can be extremely beneficial to my research," Dr Vennell ignored his comment. "Your file makes for interesting, if rather disturbing reading, but you've witnessed the dark side of human nature first-hand. Will you help me?"

"Quid pro quo?"

"Hanibal Lecter?"

"You've seen the movie too?" Smith said. "You're telling me you'll give me the all clear if I help you with your research."

"I'm giving you the all clear regardless of whether you help me or not," Dr Vennell informed him.

"Then I'll do it."

"Thank you."

"When can I go back to work?" Smith asked. "Today would be good."

This time Dr Vennell laughed. "It's not going to be today. We still have the red tape to bypass, but I'll try my best to get things moving as quickly as possible."

She stood up and offered her hand.

Smith did the same.

He shook her hand. "Thank you. Give me a shout when you need to pick my brains about my dealings with psychos."

"I'll do that," Dr Vennell said. "And thank you – I'll look forward to seeing you again."

CHAPTER NINE

Smith stopped next to his car and took out his cigarettes. He lit one and smiled. Friday the thirteenth was turning out to be a good day. His physical and mental health had been assessed and he'd passed with flying colours. His life was about to get back to normal and he was relieved. He couldn't stand the thought of having to spend another day twiddling his thumbs at home. That would be enough to truly send him round the bend.

He needed to tell Whitton the good news. He took out his phone and he was about to call her when he spotted someone walking towards him. As the man got closer Smith saw he was in a bad way. His clothes were filthy, and it looked like he hadn't washed his hair in a very long time. He was very tall, and his nose was incredibly large.

"Alright," the man said, and a waft of something foul hit Smith's nostrils.

"Morning," Smith found himself saying.

"Got any spare cash?"

"I have no idea," Smith said.

"Are you having a laugh?"

"No. I really don't have a clue if I have any cash."

Smith took out his wallet and looked inside. There was no money in it. He shouldn't have been surprised – Smith never had any cash in his wallet.

"You're out of luck," he said.

"Got a smoke then?"

"I don't know how this begging lark works," Smith said. "But I imagine you'd do a lot better if you said please and thank you once in a while."

"Please and thank you is for them that can afford it. Me, I'm not in that position."

Smith offered him the packet of cigarettes and a grubby hand reached forward and took three out. Two of those were stuck behind the man's ears.

"Got a light," he said, and added. "Please?"

Smith lit the cigarette for him. "Do you live on the streets?"

"Is it that obvious?"

"There are homeless shelters you can go to," Smith said.

"Been there, done that, got the bloody T-Shirt. Have you ever been in one of those places? You've got to have eyes in the back of your head. Sleep with one eye open if you know what I mean."

Smith had no idea what he meant.

"What's your name?"

"Henry. What's yours?"

"Jason," Smith said. "I'd better be off. Things to do."

"Me too," the man called Henry said.

With that he went on his way. Smith unlocked his car and got in. He'd forgotten all about phoning Whitton to tell her he would be back at work soon.

* * *

"I wonder how Smith's assessments went," Bridge said.

"He'll be back," DC Moore said. "Smith is like Arnie – he'll always be back."

"Let's make a start," DI Smyth said. "Arthur Miller will be arriving at one, but in the meantime, I want to discuss the cellar in the house on Nunthorpe Road."

"What's going to happen about the bloke who died in hospital?" Bridge wondered.

"We don't know. According to the doctors it was a miracle he survived as long as he did. He was severely dehydrated and many of his organs had already started to fail. Even if they had managed to save his life it was doubtful he would live for long. We have four dead men, and we have no IDs for any of them. What does this suggest?"

"Whoever locked them in there didn't want them to be identified," DC Moore put forward.

"It's possible," DI Smyth said.

"How did they even end up down there?" DC King said.

"They could have been living there for all we know," DC Moore said. "Perhaps they had a falling out with someone else in the house and they got locked in."

"It's possible whoever locked them in didn't mean to kill them," DC King suggested.

"They were left there without food or water," DC Moore reminded her. "They'd been down there for at least a week. That was no accident."

"I didn't say it was," DC King said. "I was just thinking about a book I once read. It was all about a joke that backfired in the worst possible way. A group of friends decided to play a prank on a man on his stag night. They locked him in a coffin and buried him alive."

"I'm glad I don't have friends like that," Whitton said.

"They were planning on leaving him there for an hour or so," DC King continued. "They just wanted to rattle him a bit, but then there was an accident. The van the friends were travelling in was involved in a head-on collision and all of them were killed. They were the only people who knew about the groom they'd buried alive, and the poor man was never found." DC Moore shivered. "What a horrible way to die."

"That's all very well, Kerry," DI Smyth said. "But I think it's highly unlikely that something similar happened here."

"I'm just thinking of all the logical explanations, sir," DC King said.

"I think someone did this on purpose," Whitton said. "There was a journal in the cellar – some kind of diary and the date on the front was the first of this month. It ties in roughly with when those men were imprisoned in there."

"The journal is still in the hands of Forensics," DI Smyth said. "Hopefully Webber will have figured out what language it was written in. The only part that was written in English was the date on the front. We'll take a look at it when they're finished."

"What about the room within a room?" Bridge said. "Why was one of the victims in there and why was it necessary to seal it off with a reinforced metal door?"

"We now know that the door was locked from the inside," DI Smyth said. "The man who was barely alive when he was discovered locked himself in."

"Why would he do that?" DC Moore wondered.

"I really don't know, Harry."

"I still can't understand why someone would have another room down in the cellar," Whitton said.

"That's something we'll be asking Mr Miller this afternoon," DI Smyth said. "Does anyone have any theories what this could be about? Why were those four men killed?"

"Do we know if they were drugged?" Whitton said.

"The postmortems are going to take time," DI Smyth said.

"Can I say something?" DC King said.

"Go ahead, Kerry," DI Smyth said.

"I don't think it's worth speculating on anything until we've spoken to the owner of the house. With respect, he should have been our main priority."

"You're right, and I take full responsibility for that mistake. My mind was elsewhere for a while, but I assure you I'm back and there will be no more lapses in judgment on my part."

"Is everything alright, sir?" DC King asked.

"Everything is fine."

Whitton's phone started to ring. She looked at the screen.

"It's Smith."

She answered the phone and put it on speaker. She told Smith as much.

"I'm back on the team." Smith came straight to the point.

"Glad to hear it," DI Smyth told him.

"How did you manage to pull that off?" Bridge said. "Did it involve bribes?"

"I'll have you know there is nothing wrong with my physical and mental wellbeing," Smith said.

"Your mental health history could keep psychologists busy for years."

"That's exactly what the shrink said," Smith told him. "I just thought I'd give you all the good news."

"When can you return to work?" DI Smyth said.

"I'm already back. I've just arrived at Nunthorpe Road."

"What on earth are you doing in Scarcroft?"

"I need to have another look around the house, boss."

"Hold your horses," DI Smyth said. "You're not officially back on duty, are you?"

"It didn't stop me yesterday."

"Smith, what exactly are you looking for?"

"Sorry, boss," Smith said. "You're breaking up. The reception is terrible round here."

CHAPTER TEN

Smith put the phone back in his pocket and looked once more at the outside of number 12 Nunthorpe Road. The road looked very different today and the only clue to indicate that this was a crime scene was the police tape that had sealed off the property. Smith's car was the only one parked on the road – the ambulance was long gone, as were the patrol cars and the vehicles belonging to the detectives on the team.

Smith needed to take a second look for this very reason. He needed to take in the scene without the distraction of the frenzied activities of his colleagues. Perhaps the house would talk to him now. It might be more willing to spill its secrets in a one-on-one conversation.

Smith ducked under the tape telling the public that entry was prohibited, and he walked up the path to the front door. Baldwin had told him that PC Black had been given the tedious task of preventing anyone from entering the house and Smith was glad. PC Black owed him a few favours and he would let him inside the house without asking too many questions.

"Sarge," PC Black said. "Are you back at work?"

"As of now, I am," Smith told him. "Physical and psych evaluations all good. I need to take another look inside."

"No problem."

"How long have you been here?" Smith asked him.

"A couple of hours."

"Anything happening?"

"Not a sausage," PC Black said. "What exactly happened in there?"

"That's what I'm going to find out. Is the house open?"

PC Black rummaged in his pocket and pulled out a bunch of keys.

"The owner of the house gave us the spare set."

Smith took them. "Thanks, Jim. I'm not to be disturbed."

"Right you are, Sarge."

Smith unlocked the door and went inside the house. The smell of death still lingered, and Smith knew it would be here for a very long time. The funk of decay and decomposition would cling to the curtains and attach itself to the carpets and no amount of scrubbing would ever completely wipe it out. He walked down the hallway and stopped next to the door that opened onto the staircase down to the cellar. He walked past it towards the kitchen. He would take a look in the cellar last.

The kitchen hadn't been used in a while – that much was clear. There were no plates, cups or knives and forks in the sink. In fact, the only thing in there were some old stains. The worktops were covered in dust. Smith opened the fridge and saw that there was nothing in there either. The handle still had evidence of fingerprint powder on it and Smith deduced that Webber had done a very thorough job in here.

He left the kitchen and went into the living room. The old furniture had seen better days. The fabric on the three-seater was badly torn and there were numerous dubious stains on it. The carpet looked like it hadn't been cleaned in years. Smith found a similar scene in the two small bedrooms on the ground floor. This house wasn't fit for habitation, and he wondered what the owner was planning on doing with it.

He checked upstairs. There were three further bedrooms on the second floor and another box room on the top storey of the house. There was a bed in that one, but very little else. Whoever the men in the cellar were Smith didn't think they'd been living in the house.

He went back downstairs and stopped outside the entrance to the cellar again. He really didn't want to go down there, but he knew it had to be done. He found a door wedge in the kitchen and secured it under the cellar door just to be on the safe side. He didn't want to get trapped down there.

He took out his phone, activated the torch app and made his way down the stairs into the darkness.

He reached the bottom step, and something occurred to him. It would be very difficult to get four grown men down here unless they were threatened with something, or they went down willingly. He made a mental note to bring this up with the team.

It was very warm down in the bowels of the house and Smith couldn't understand why that was. In his experience, cellars were cold, damp places – hot air had a tendency to flow upwards, so why was it so balmy down here?

There was a bathroom of sorts opposite the bottom of the stairs. Smith hadn't paid it much attention when he was first here. It wasn't a proper room – it was more of a partitioned section of the cellar. Inside was a toilet, a sink and a small bathtub. Smith found himself placing a hand on the tap on the sink. He turned it but nothing happened. It was the same with both of the taps on the bath. There was no running water down here.

The reinforced metal door was still where it had been left after Webber had removed it. Smith walked past it towards the room where the man was found on the bed. The beam from his phone wasn't a great source of light but it was all he had. He cursed himself for not bringing a torch with him. He wondered why there were no lights in the cellar and decided that it was possible the cellar was a later addition to the property and the owner hadn't got round to connecting the electricity.

This theory was dispelled when he pointed the phone at the ceiling in the hidden room and spotted the light fitting. There was a single bulb but Smith couldn't find the switch anywhere. He shone the beam of the phone around the room but there wasn't much to see. The blister pack of tablets that had been on the bedside table were gone. Webber had informed him they were paracetamol pills of the type you could purchase anywhere. The journal had also been taken away for analysis. Smith knew that Webber would have figured out what language it was written in by now.

"Why was that particular man in here?" he asked the bare walls. He wondered if all four men were down here for the same amount of time. And if so, what were they doing here? No matter how much he thought about it he couldn't come up with a logical reason why four men had to die of dehydration in the darkest depths of a house in York.

The torch on his phone flickered and the screen told Smith his phone battery was running low. It was time to get the hell out of the cellar. Smith turned away from the bed, and shone the light at the empty doorway. He'd put one foot out of the room when he saw it. There was something on the wall next to the doorframe. The beam of the torch was getting dimmer, but Smith could just make out the series of scratches on the wall. When he examined them more closely, he realised they weren't scratches – they were notches etched into the paint on the wall.

Smith turned off the torch and opened his camera. The only light inside the room came from the screen of the phone. Smith snapped blindly. He took a number of photographs of the strange notches in the wall. A flashing light on the top of the phone told him the battery was about to die. Smith stepped into the cellar – the screen of the phone went out and he was left in absolute blackness.

CHAPTER ELEVEN

Billie Jones was experiencing a deep sense of unease. The journal found in the hidden room in the cellar of number 12 Nunthorpe Road had captured her attention as soon as she'd set eyes on it and she'd been able to concentrate on nothing else since it was discovered. The language within was something familiar but it wasn't anything she could remember coming across before.

She'd eventually figured out the language purely by chance. There was a date written on the front page of the journal – 1st March, but thereafter the month of March didn't appear. It had been replaced with the word *Mars*. It wasn't difficult to figure out what it meant, and after a quick search her suspicions were confirmed. It was a common word for the month of March. After keying a few more of the words into Google Translate Billie found her starting point – the journal was written in Albanian, and with the help of the translation program she was able to read the rest of it.

It made for disturbing reading. The narrative within the diary was truly horrific and some parts of it made Billie feel physically sick to the extent that she was forced to take a break from the haunting tale the author of the diary had told.

The four men found dead in the cellar were all Albanian. There was nothing to indicate how they ended up down in the cellar and, so far Billie couldn't find anything to indicate who was responsible for their incarceration. The tone of the journal was more upbeat at the beginning. There was talk of food and water and the author didn't mention anything about the lights not working.

That came later. On March 7th the ominous word was written in block capitals.

ERRESIRE: Darkness.

There was another word that didn't need any translation – *Pandemi*. Billie couldn't figure out the significance of this particular word. Why was an Albanian man talking about a pandemic?

The food ran out the day after the darkness became a constant feature down in the cellar, and the men had used up all of the water two days after that. Billie shivered. They'd arrived just too late. These men had gone without water for three days, and it's possible their lives could have been spared if the call from the owner of the house had come in a day earlier.

Billie was no handwriting expert, but it was clear that the majority of the journal had been composed by the same scribe. The writing was very distinctive. Someone else had taken over on March 10th and when Billie translated the first thing the new author had written the reason for this became apparent.

Ardit ka vdekur.

"Ardit is dead," Billie read the translation out loud.

She didn't need to read to the end to know how this particular tale concluded. She'd seen it first-hand. She copied the whole translated text, pasted it onto a new Word document and sent it as an attachment to DI Smyth. She also printed a copy. She knew from experience that Smith would prefer to read this on paper. While she waited for the printer to spit out the story of an unimaginable horror, she went to find Webber. She needed to tell him what she'd found.

* * *

Dr Kenny Bean was experiencing a similar sensation of nausea. The experienced Head of Pathology had seen his fair share of horrific things in his career but what he was looking at now was something he was not likely to forget for a very long time.

The unidentified men had been stripped and placed on the metal tables earlier and Dr Bean's eyes were drawn to the wounds on their arms, legs and torsos straight away. He'd never seen anything like them. There were deep, jagged lacerations all over three of the men's bodies. Dr Bean had been given the back story behind the deaths of the four men and it didn't take him long to deduce the cause of death for all four of them. The evidence of severe dehydration was obvious, but the wounds he was looking at were puzzling.

Dr Bean had ascertained that three of the men died in stages ranging from two days ago to as early as yesterday. One of them had perished hours before he was found. His initial thoughts on the times of death had been wrong. The men hadn't been dead as long as he first assumed, and this was due to the effects of severe dehydration. Three of the men displayed deterioration similar to that of a week-old corpse. The fourth man was alive but he died later in hospital. Dr Bean couldn't detect any sign of the injuries his friends had been subjected to on his body and this was very strange.

He took a number of close-up photographs of the wounds and got to work. The lacerations were similar in size and depth and there was clear evidence that they'd been sustained very recently. It would take a more thorough examination to determine the time scale involved but Dr Bean estimated it had been in the past few days. This had happened while the men were held prisoners in the cellar.

The ping of his phone interrupted Dr Bean's train of thought. He'd received a message. He swiped the screen and saw it was from Smith. He smiled when he read what Smith had written.

Do you have anything interesting to tell me?

Dr Bean typed a short reply telling Smith he might have something very interesting, and sent it off. He would leave Smith hanging for a while.

He put down his phone and turned his attention back to the mysterious wounds on three of the men. He picked up a tape and set about measuring the lacerations. All of them were of similar length. The depth of the wounds were more or less the same too.

Dr Bean looked closely at the pale body of the man on the table at the end.

"Why did you come away unscathed?" he asked the corpse. "What makes you so special?"

The man's eyes were open, and they were already filming over. It didn't take long for that to happen. His mouth was open, revealing an uneven row of teeth. One of the front teeth was missing. Dr Bean looked at the man's mouth and then his gaze found one of the wounds on the arm of one of his friends. He could feel the bile rising in his throat. He swallowed a few times and picked up his phone.

The absence of the blue dots told him Smith hadn't read the message yet. Dr Bean was glad – he had something new to add to it.

Here's something for you to think about, he wrote. *How much do you know about cannibals?*

This time the blue dots appeared straight away and the phone told him Smith was composing a reply. It didn't take long. Dr Bean read the message and sighed.

I haven't smoked cannabis for ages.

Dr Bean's next message left little to the imagination.

The man you found in the hidden room survived for as long as he did because he was eating his friends.

Smith had read the message, but he didn't reply to it.

CHAPTER TWELVE

"Interview with Arthur Miller commenced, 13:23," DI Smyth said. "Present, Mr Miller, DI Smyth and DS Whitton. Mr Miller has waived his right to legal representation."

"You told me this was just an informal chat," Arthur said. "You said I'm not in any trouble."

"For the record," DI Smyth said. "Mr Miller is here of his own free will. Thank you for coming in. You own a house in Scarcroft – number 12 Nunthorpe Road. Is that correct."

"That's right. I have a few properties in the city."

"Do you rent these properties out?" Whitton asked.

"I do."

"When we were at the aforementioned house," DI Smyth said. "It didn't look like it was fit for habitation."

"I'm still busy fixing it up."

"How long have you owned number 12?" Whitton said.

"About two years."

"That's quite a long time to spend fixing up a house," DI Smyth said.

"I haven't always been doing it up," Arthur said. "I've had tenants in there in the past."

"When was the last time you let the house out?" Whitton said.

"A couple of months ago."

"You called us yesterday," DI Smyth said. "You phoned in about the three dead men in the cellar. You went to the house because you believed there to be squatters living in there."

"They're a real problem," Arthur said. "And the freeloading scum are impossible to get rid of. They've got rights – can you believe it."

"What were you planning on doing yesterday?" Whitton said. "You arrived at the house with four other men. What were your plans?"

"I was going to persuade the squatters to get out of my house. It's my property – what gives someone the right to move into my house? How would you like it if you came home to find someone living in your place?"

"We're not here to talk about me," Whitton said.

"When did you realise something was wrong?" DI Smyth asked.

"When I saw the padlock on the cellar door," Arthur said.

"You didn't put the padlock there?" Whitton said.

"Of course not. Why would I padlock an interior door?"

"What did you do then?" DI Smyth said.

"I had some bolt cutters in the car," Arthur said. "So I went to get them and I cut the padlock off. It's not against the law to break into a room in your own house, is it?"

"Not as far as I'm aware. What did you do then?"

"I almost puked," Arthur told him. "That's what I did. That smell – God, it was awful. I flicked the light switch, but nothing happened."

"Are you saying there are lights in the cellar?" Whitton said.

"Of course. There aren't any windows down there."

"But the lights weren't working?" DI Smyth said.

"That's right. But I had a torch in the car, so I went to get it."

"You seem to be very prepared for every eventuality," Whitton said. "Bolt cutters and a torch."

"Tools of the trade."

"Can you explain some more about the cellar?" DI Smyth said.

"What is there to say?" Arthur asked.

"Was the cellar already there when you purchased the property?"

"Of course it was."

"Why is there another room down there?" Whitton said. "What's that room used for?"

"I think the previous owner used it for storage."

"The reinforced door is a bit over the top, isn't it?" DI Smyth said.

"You'll have to ask the old owner about that," Arthur said. "I'll be happy to give you her details."

"That would be appreciated. Do you know why the room is soundproofed?"

"That's another thing you'll need to ask the previous owner about."

"When was the last time you went to number 12 Nunthorpe Road?" Whitton said.

"A couple of weeks ago."

"Is it usual for you not to visit your properties for so long?" DI Smyth asked.

"I own four houses," Arthur said. "They take up a lot of my time and I don't check on the ones I'm not renting out very often."

"So yesterday was the first time you'd been inside number 12 for a couple of weeks?" DI Smyth said. "Around about the start of the month then?"

"Probably the end of last month. Like I said, I'm a busy man."

"When did you realise there were squatters in number 12?" Whitton said.

"Yesterday," Arthur replied.

"And yet you came prepared," DI Smyth said. "With backup in place. That doesn't make any sense."

"I heard a rumour there were people living in the house, so I took some friends with me. It makes perfect sense to me."

"Where did you hear this rumour?" Whitton said.

"From Mrs Pratt next door. I heard her talking to Mr Ali at the corner shop about it."

"Mrs Pratt didn't tell you herself?"

"We don't really get on," Arthur said. "Look, I've been more than cooperative. I was the one who called you yesterday. I'm here now, aren't I? When will I be allowed to go back inside my own house?"

"I'm afraid the house is off limits," DI Smyth said. "It's a crime scene and it will remain as such until we get some answers."

"You're not going to get them from me."

"Have you had problems with squatters in the past?" Whitton said.

"On and off," Arthur told her. "When you're a landlord they're an occupational hazard, if you'll pardon the pun. What exactly happened to those people? Nobody has told me anything. All I know is that they died. I need to know when I'll be able to get my house back."

DI Smyth cast a glance at Whitton and received a subtle nod of the head in reply. It was clear they weren't going to get anything useful from Arthur Miller today. DI Smyth indicated as much for the record and told him he was free to go.

CHAPTER THIRTEEN

Smith's eyes were glued to his phone. He was reading the message from Kenny Bean for the fiftieth time.

The man you found in the hidden room survived for as long as he did because he was eating his friends.

Smith had known the peculiar Head of Pathology for quite some time and he wasn't a man to fool around. If Dr Bean thought the man found in the hidden room had been partaking in cannibalism he had to take him at his word.

The idea made Smith feel sick. It didn't bear thinking what could possibly make a man do that. What must have been going through his head at the time? Was his survival instinct so strong that he could consider something so abhorrent? Smith didn't know. All he knew was if he were ever in a similar predicament, he wouldn't be able to do the same.

He tried to put together a series of events in his head. The three men in the cellar itself had died first – that much was clear, but when had the other man made the decision to eat them? Smith didn't know much about the human anatomy, but he guessed there wouldn't be much nutritional value in the flesh of a severely dehydrated human being.

He pushed the concept of cannibalism out of his head and thought back to the strange notches on the wall of the hidden room. He'd stuck his phone on charge as soon as he got back to his car, and it was now charging further in the kitchen. He swiped the screen and brought up his photographs. He selected the most recent ones and hoped it had captured the notches properly.

The photo wasn't great – the image was rather blurred, but Smith could still make out the mysterious scratches. He'd seen something like them before. They were all similar in shape and size. Four vertical lines had been dissected by one diagonal line. It was a series of sets of five, but there was no way to tell what the notches were symbolising. Was it five days? Five hours? Smith didn't know.

The phone started to ring and Billie Jones' name appeared on the screen. "Billie," Smith answered it. "What can I do for you?"

"It's more what I can do for you," she said. "The dead men in the cellar were Albanian. I translated the journal and it's a horrific tale."

"So I'm starting to believe. Is there anything in there about cannibalism?"

"What?"

"Does it mention anything about the men eating each other?" Smith said.

"Good God, no. Where did that come from?"

"Dr Bean," Smith told her. "He found indications to show that one of the men developed a taste for human flesh while he was down there."

"There's nothing about cannibalism in the journal."

"I suppose it's not something you'd want to document," Smith decided.

"I've printed out a copy of the translation," Billie said. "I thought you'd prefer to read a printed version."

"I appreciate it," Smith said. "Although I'm not sure I really want to read it."

"Where are you?"

"At home. I've just got back from Nunthorpe Road."

"What were you doing in Scarcroft?" Billie asked.

"I needed to take another look at the cellar."

"I'm on my lunch break," Billie said. "I can drop the translation off if you like."

"That would be great."

"I'll be there in ten minutes," Billie said and rang off.

"The plot thickens," Smith told Theakston.

The overweight Bull Terrier was perched at his feet and the loud snorts coming from his mouth were telling Smith he wasn't listening.

Smith shifted the deadweight of the dog off his feet and got up to go outside. He needed a cigarette. He'd only smoked three today and he felt good about it.

The smoke drifting over the fence told Smith that his next-door-neighbour had had the same idea. Sheila Rogers was at the fence before Smith had even had the chance to close the back door.

"Afternoon," she said. "Are you still off work?"

Smith lit a cigarette. "Not for much longer. What about you – day off?"

"I told them to stick the job up their arse. I hated it anyway, and I'm starting at Fran's school after Easter anyway."

"You got the teaching assistant job?"

"They called me yesterday," Sheila said. "I was supposed to be informed a lot sooner than that, but there was a mix-up with HR. Anyway, I got the job, and I phoned the Post Office straight away. It felt amazing."

"Congratulations."

"Thanks. The money's not that great, but at least I'll have more time off with Fran, and there's no weekend work."

A dog started to bark inside the house. It was Fred. The ugly Pug's unmistakable high-pitched yelp told Smith Billie Jones was at the door. He stubbed out his cigarette and said goodbye to his strange neighbour.

* * *

"What is this place?"

Marcus Green scanned the room he was in. The walls were bare. They were devoid of any paintings, photographs and other decorations people generally liked to use to brighten up the inside of a house. A single-seater leather chair was the only piece of furniture in the room.

"This is still a work in progress," the woman told him.

Marcus hadn't given her offer a second thought when she'd made it. He still had most of the three-hundred pounds she'd given him yesterday and he hadn't expected her to come back. But come back she did and the story she told grabbed Marcus's attention instantly. She needed someone to take part in a very important social experiment – Marucs would be paid well for participating and all he had to do was move into the woman's house and document his existence there in a journal. He would be fed, watered and given a roof over his head. As far as jobs went, this was a great gig.

"You won't be living up here," the man added.

Marcus still hadn't made up his mind about him. The woman had a warm, motherly air about her but the man was much colder. And the face mask he wore was somewhat unsettling. Marcus didn't know then that this would be the norm in the coming months. Soon, it would be the people without masks who would stand out in a crowd.

"Come on," the woman said. "Let me show you to your quarters."

She left the room and walked down a narrow hallway. Marcus followed her. They stopped next to a door at the end. The woman opened it and flicked a light switch. Marcus leaned forward and looked inside.

"Whoa. What is this?"

"Your new home," the woman said. "Come on, follow me."

She started to walk down the stairs. Marcus paused for a moment and followed after her.

"Take a seat," she gestured to the three-piece suite against one of the walls.

It looked brand new. Opposite it was a widescreen TV. A number of games consoles stood on a cabinet below. Marcus sat on the three-seater. The woman sat down next to him.

"There are a number of things I need to make clear," she said. "What you are about to take part in is of paramount importance to the future of your fellow man. Do you understand?"

Marcus told her he did even though he had no idea what she meant. If he was going to get paid to sit on his arse and play video games for a few days he wasn't going to make any waves.

"Are you absolutely certain nobody will miss you for a while?"

It wasn't the first time she'd asked him this. Marcus couldn't understand why it was so important.

"My loving parents stopped trying to find me a long time ago," he said. "And street life is hardly conducive to making close friends."

"You sound like an educated man."

"Once upon a time," Marcus said. "I quit the medical degree in my final year. I chose a life of freedom over the rat race of the medical profession."

"A very noble decision. There is a bathroom off to the side. It's small but it's ample for your needs. You will sleep in here – is that going to be a problem?"

"I've slept in worst places," Marcus told her.

"There is food in the pantry," the woman carried on. "It's mostly freeze-dried but for the experiment to work that's how it has to be."

"What exactly is this experiment?"

"That doesn't concern you. Your part is simple. You remain down here and document everything you experience in the journal on the table."

She pointed to the A4 sized book.

"Can I take a look around?" Marcus asked.

"There will be plenty of time for that. Do we have a deal, mister homeless man?"

Marcus held out his hand. "I believe we do."

The woman didn't shake the hand. "It's better if we keep contact to the bare minimum. You'll start to understand that when the others arrive."

This was clearly news to Marcus. "Others?"

"I'll let you get settled in."

She got up and ascended the stairs before Marcus could stop her. He heard the door slam and then he heard a loud click as the bolt on the other side of the door was slid into place.

CHAPTER FOURTEEN

Billie Jones was fighting off the affections of two boisterous dogs. Smith had never seen Theakston and Fred so excited about a visitor. The Bull Terrier and the Pug usually had a casual sniff and that was it, but Webber's assistant was clearly having an effect on the two dogs. Smith had never seen anything like it before.

"I apologise for them." he said. "They have no manners."

Billie laughed. "It's alright – I love dogs."

"And they obviously like you. I've never seen them do this before. If I didn't know any better I'd say they were in love. Bridge had better watch out. Do you want some coffee?"

"I'd love some. I don't have to be back for another forty-five minutes."

Smith made them both some coffee and asked her if they'd made any more progress.

"The journal was bugging me," Billie said. "Why would someone keep a diary of their time locked up in a cellar?"

"Why indeed?" Smith agreed. "Does the journal give us any idea who these men are?"

"There are some words in there that Google Translate didn't recognise, and I think that's because they're names. Ardit is one I can recall."

"Ardit," Smith repeated. "Why does that name ring a bell?"

He'd heard it before but he couldn't remember where. He took a sip of his coffee and it occurred to him.

"Ardit Gashi," he said out of the blue.

"Do you think it's the same man?"

"Impossible," Smith told her. "Ardit Gashi was murdered almost fifteen years ago. Together with his brother. It was one of my first murder cases back when I was still a DC. Two brothers were found dead in the house they rented. I remember the case because it was one of those little buggers who started the ball rolling."

He nodded to Theakston. The portly Bull Terrier was now gazing up at Billie with doe eyes.

"A neighbour called in about the dog," Smith carried on. "The poor thing wouldn't stop barking. The house was a mess – all dog shit and filth. We found Ardit and his brother when we went to check it out. They'd got themselves involved with some dangerous people and they ended up dead because of it."

"You've got a good memory for past investigations," Billie said.

"I remember all of them. I don't know if that's a gift or a curse. What else do we know? Apart from what's in the diary I mean?"

"The reinforced metal door can only be locked from the inside."

"Isn't that unusual?" Smith wondered.

"Extremely. We're still busy analysing the locking mechanism, but I've never seen a door that can only be locked from the inside. I don't know what it means."

"It means someone went to great lengths to make sure nobody could get in from the outside without destroying the door," Smith said. "But I still can't think of why someone would install a door like that."

"The electricity and the water were both off," Billie said. "Webber found the shut off valve for the water and someone had turned it off manually. Same with the electricity. The mains switch was down on the DB board."

"Perhaps the owner did it," Smith suggested.

"Did he mention anything about it in the interview?"

"I'll have to ask Whitton. This is a really baffling one."

Billie's phone beeped. She swiped the screen and smiled.

"It's Rupert."

Smith smiled too. "Do you realise, since I've known Bridge, you're the only person who has been allowed to call him Rupert. It must be serious."

"Hmm," Billie said. "I'd better get back. Thanks for the coffee."

"Thanks for dropping the journal round," Smith said.

He decided to add to his cigarette tally for the day before reading the innocuous looking sheets of paper on the kitchen table. He knew he needed to read the last words of two of the Albanian men, but he decided it wouldn't hurt to put it off for another five minutes or so.

After the smoke, he made himself another cup of coffee and sat down to read. The date on the front was: March 1st 2020. Billie had added a note explaining that this part of the diary had been written in English. Smith turned the page and started to read.

1st March 2020.

The place isn't as bad as some of them. Busar has expressed some concerns about the locked cellar door, but Erjon rationalized it by suggesting the implications of being discovered necessitate it. Busar seemed to accept this.

Smith stood up and walked over to the drawer next to the fridge. There was a notepad and a pen in there. He took them out and returned to the table. He wrote the names, *Ardit*, *Erjon* and *Busar* on it. Then he added a comment. The language in the diary was unusual. This wasn't the work of an Albanian peasant. The author of the journal was clearly an educated man.

He carried on reading.

Flamur has already made it clear he will be monopolizing the Xbox. This is not up for debate. Some of the games he plays seem inappropriate given the circumstances but perhaps that is part of the experiment Mother talked about.

Smith picked up the pen and wrote, Flamur's name beneath the other three.

"Mother," he said out loud.

He wrote this down too.

65

The first day passed quickly, the diarist continued. *Erjon suggested watching television and after some persuasion Flamur relinquished the games console, but it was a fruitless exercise. The television set is not connected to any of the networks. There will be no TV in this cellar.*

Mother cautioned us about the food. The pantry is full but it has to be used sensibly. Greed will come with consequences, she said. Water consumption too is to be monitored carefully. None of us paid her much attention. The rewards are great. Flamur plans to use his share to travel back to Albania. He talks of very little else. Even when he's dismembering zombies he's making plans to return home dressed like a king.

Time is an unknown quantity down here. There are no clocks – Mother took our watches and she insisted we leave our phones behind. She told us that was very important in order for the experiment to work. There are no windows and with the absence of natural light we have only the internal body clock to tell us whether it's night or day. I believe that too will become unreliable soon.

Busar drinks too much water. Mother warned him about it but he drinks nevertheless. The taps in the bathroom and on the sink in the kitchenette will never run dry, he reminds us.

That was all there was on the first day. Smith didn't know what to make of it, but he did know they had a number of things to look into. They had the first names of the dead men and they had someone the men referred to as *Mother*.

CHAPTER FIFTEEN

"Mother," DI Smyth said.

He wrote it on the whiteboard in the small conference room.

"Who is this mother?" he added.

"It's probably a woman," DC Moore stated the obvious.

"Thank you for that, Harry," DI Smyth said. "Any thoughts?"

"She's offered them a lot of money to take part in this experiment," Whitton said. "The writer of the diary spoke of Flamur's plans to go back to Albania afterwards."

"That's how they were persuaded to go down there," DC King suggested. "It's possible these men got an offer too good to refuse. Why else would someone volunteer to be locked in a cellar?"

"I don't buy it." It was DC Moore. "I don't care how much money someone offered me, there is no way I would volunteer to be locked in a cellar."

"That's because you're lucky, Harry," Bridge told him. "You were brought up in a system where very few people have to suffer. You got a good education, and this enabled you to land a decent job. You don't have to stress about where your next meal is coming from, and you never will."

"Nice speech, Sarge," DC Moore said. "It's not my fault I was born here."

"That's enough," DI Smyth said. "Bridge is right. It's highly likely these men are illegal immigrants. There are more of them here than we think, and many of them know nothing of the privileges we take for granted. They come from poverty, and they arrive here with high expectations, only to find out this is not the land of milk and honey they expected it to be. Then someone comes along and offers them probably more money than they've ever earned in their lives. All they have to do is agree to be locked in a cellar for a while. They're promised food and water – a substantial amount of cash, and all they have to do is wait it out."

"But things didn't turn out quite how they expected them to turn out," DC King said.

"No, Kerry," DI Smyth said. "No, they didn't."

"At least we now have IDs for them," DC Moore said.

"We have first names only," Bridge pointed out. "And we don't know if those are their real names."

"I think they will be," DC King said. "I don't think the author of the diary would use fake names in the journal."

"It's still not going to help us find out anything about them," Whitton said. "If they're illegals it will be impossible to find out how long they've been here, and where they've been since they arrived."

"What about the asylum centres?" DC King suggested. "They might have spent some time at one of them."

"It's a long shot," DI Smyth said. "A very long shot."

"What about the Albanian community?" DC Moore said. "The immigrants tend to stick together. What if we put some feelers out there?"

"That's an even longer shot, Harry," Whitton told him. "We've dealt with the minority communities before and they're notoriously wary of the police. With good reason too. Some of these people have suffered at the hands of law enforcement and they just don't trust us."

"The journal was more of the same for the first week or so," DI Smyth changed tack. "Days rolled into night, but things changed last week."

"The lights were turned off," DC King said. "And the food and water ran out."

"Right," DI Smyth said. "Somehow the running water in the cellar was disconnected and the electricity was turned off. Why did that happen?"

"Do you think it was part of this experiment?" DC King put forward.

"What kind of experiment are we talking about?" DC Moore asked. "What could someone even learn from locking a bunch of blokes in a cellar and depriving them of food, water and light?"

"The sickest kind of experiment," Bridge said. "Perhaps we're dealing with a sadist. Someone who gets off on watching people suffer."

"I don't buy it, Sarge," DC King said. "Forensics didn't find any hidden cameras down there. Surely if this was the work of someone who gains sadistic pleasure out of seeing people suffer, they'd want to watch it."

"I think that's what the journal was supposed to be about," Whitton said.

"How did the writer of the diary carry on when the lights went out?" DC King wondered.

DC Moore frowned at her. "You're weird."

"Our eyes adjust to the darkness," Bridge said. "It's how they're designed. Those men will have adapted and after a while they'll have been able to make out shapes down there."

"And how did the author of the diary know what day it was?" DC King asked.

"You really are weird," DC Moore commented.

"There are no lights down there, Harry," DC King elaborated. "How did they know what day it was? After a while you wouldn't even know if it was day or night."

"The final few entries make for very disturbing reading," DI Smyth carried on. "Three of the Albanian men are dead and the remaining man takes over the narration."

"Flamur," DC King elaborated. "He was the one locked in the hidden room."

"We can ascertain from the journal the order in which the men perished," DI Smyth said. "But there is nothing in there to explain why the fourth victim locked himself inside that room."

"Perhaps he was worried about Mother," DC King suggested.

"It's possible," Whitton agreed. "We know the door can only be locked from the inside. Maybe Flamur locked himself in to protect himself from this *Mother*."

"There's no mention of cannibalism in the diary," DC Moore said. "Dr Bean found evidence to suggest that Flamur had been eating his compatriots."

"I don't think that's something you'd want to own up to, Harry," Bridge said. "If I'd been chomping on the flesh of my mates, I'd keep it very quiet."

"Very reassuring," Whitton said.

"Did Pathology find anything else?" DC King asked.

"Dr Bean is still busy with the bodies," DI Smyth said.

His phoned beeped on the table in front of him. He swiped the screen, read the message and suddenly felt very ill. The building nausea had nothing to do with the idea of flesh-eating Albanians.

The message was short and straight to the point.

You've got two days to pay up. You know what happens if you don't.

CHAPTER SIXTEEN

Smith had been unsure what to do. The message DI Smyth had forwarded him left little doubt about the intentions of the sender, but the additional message the DI had added also made it clear that he didn't want his predicament out in the open just yet. He needed time to think.

Smith was halfway through his fourth coffee of the day and his mind had been working at double speed. The man who thought he could blackmail a detective inspector had to be stopped but the only way Smith could think of doing that would involve betraying a confidence. The blackmailer had been foolish enough to send the message without taking the precaution of withholding his number. It was clear he thought DI Smyth would give in to his demands without a fight, but this was going to cost him. Smith knew there were ways to find the owner of the phone the message was sent from but he would need help. He couldn't do it on his own. He was facing a moral dilemma. He was determined to make the blackmailer pay for this, but he wasn't sure if the DI would thank him for it.

"Fuck it."

He'd stubbed out his cigarette and immediately lit another. He would try and smoke less tomorrow. He'd opened his phone and called Baldwin.

She'd called back less than an hour later with a name and an address. Baldwin never ceased to amaze him. Smith didn't know where she sourced her information and he never asked. Her somewhat unorthodox resources had proved to be invaluable in the past and she was an essential part of the team.

The address surprised Smith. DI Smyth had flown almost six thousand miles to meet up with a man who lived a stone's throw from York. The man who believed he could get away with blackmailing Smith's boss lived thirty miles down the A64 on the outskirts of Leeds.

Michael Teasdale was twenty-nine. Baldwin told Smith that he owned a property in the village of Fenton, five miles east of the city centre. According to the records Baldwin had managed to gain access to he was currently unemployed and had been for the past few years. The house he owned was paid for and as Smith entered the village he was left in little doubt where the funds had come from. The houses here were expensive and it would be impossible for an unemployed man to be able to afford one. Smith wondered how many times he'd pulled off the scam DI Smyth had fallen for. It didn't matter – his blackmailing days were over.

Smith turned onto Main Street and looked out for number 22. He passed an old-fashioned pub and a village hall and slowed down when he came to a cluster of houses. Number 22 was a detached cottage a couple of hundred metres further down the road. Smith parked his car behind a blue 4x4 and turned off the engine. He'd rehearsed how he was going to tackle Michael Teasdale on the drive down, but he needed a moment to get everything straight in his head. He had to make damn sure that this was going to work.

Smoke was oozing out of the chimney of the cottage. There wasn't a puff of breeze, and the smoke was rising straight up. Someone was home. Smith walked up the path to the front door and pressed the bell. The door was opened shortly afterwards by the man Smith recognised from the damning photographs DI Smyth had shown him. Michael Teasdale looked much paler now. His tan hadn't lasted very long.

"Mr Teasdale?" Smith said.

Michael looked him up and down and if Smith didn't know any better, he would think he was being appraised. Was Michael on the lookout for another victim.

"Who are you?" he asked.

Smith took out his ID and flashed it in front of Michael's face. He did it quickly but that was intentional.

"Jason Smith," Smith said. "I'm with HMRC."

"Never heard of them," Michael said.

"I'm aware of that. That's why I'm here. Can I come inside? It really would be better to discuss this in private."

"What's this all about? And what's this HMRS?"

"HMRC," Smith corrected. "Her Majesty's Revenue and Customs. You were informed of this visit beforehand."

"I didn't get anything."

"I assure you the correspondence was sent out. You're not obliged to let me in but I would advise against refusing. As of now we're at the informal chat stage, and I assure you, you do not want to go the formal route."

"I suppose you'd better come in then."

Smith made himself comfortable in the living room. The leather lounge suite looked expensive, and the television attached to the wall was the latest model. There was a fireplace below the TV. The logs were piled high, and the heat was stifling.

"Do you live alone?" Smith asked Michael.

"That's right. What is it you want from me?"

Smith took out his phone and pretended to look at something on the screen.

"According to our records," he said. "You haven't paid income tax for three years. Is that correct?"

"I've been out of work for a while," Michael explained.

"I see. Do you claim benefits?"

"I don't bother."

"Why is that?" Smith said.

"Because I'd probably qualify for a couple of quid a week in Universal Credit. I own this place outright and I have savings in the bank."

"Therein lies the problem," Smith said. "Again, according to our records there has been no tax paid on these assets. Where did the money come from?"

"I inherited it."

Smith looked him in the eye. Michael turned his head to the side.

"There is nothing in our system about that," Smith said. "But it'll be easy enough to rectify. Inheritance is easy to trace."

"It was a relative in Australia." Michael said this so quickly it was obviously a lie.

"Go on," Smith urged.

"And I kept the money there," Michael added. "I only brought it over to pay for this place."

Smith had heard enough. He got to his feet and walked over to the television. He didn't know much about modern TVs, but if he did he would realise this was a Samsung Neon 77-inch set that cost over six thousand pounds. He turned back around to face Michael Teasdale.

"Tax evasion is serious, Mr Teasdale."

"I didn't know I had to pay tax on an inheritance," Michael said. "I really didn't know."

"It's easily fixed. What we'll need from you is this: you'll have to fill out some forms, and submit them with the relevant supporting documents. A copy of the proof of inheritance will suffice."

"Is that really necessary? Can't I just pay up? I don't mind paying whatever fine I need to pay. I've got some money coming in. In a couple of days, I'll have enough to settle my tax bill."

Smith remained silent. He wanted to let Michael Teasdale stew for a bit.

"Tax evasion is serious," he repeated after a while had passed. "But it's not as serious as blackmail."

"What?"

"Shut up. Blackmail. According to the Theft Act of 1968, Section 21 the definition of blackmail is when a person with a view to gain for themselves makes an unwarranted demand intending to cause loss to another. Does that sound familiar?"

"I don't know what you're talking about," Michael said, but the change in his body language suggested otherwise.

"Blackmail carries a maximum sentence of fourteen years, Michael."

"What do you want from me?"

"You fucked up, Michael," Smith said. "You picked the wrong target in Thailand."

"I really don't know what you're talking about."

"This money you're expecting," Smith said. "Where exactly is it coming from?"

"Does it matter?"

"It does when it involves a good friend of mine. Oliver Smyth. Does that name ring any bells?"

"Should it?"

Smith turned to look at the fire. "You should really have a fireguard on there. It would be a shame for a rogue spark to catch the carpet. This place would burn down in no time."

"Are you threatening me now?"

Smith nodded his head. "I already have enough to justify hauling you in and interrogating you until you can't take any more. Do you really want that? Do you really want to take your chances with police officers when they find out you've tried to blackmail one of their own? It won't end well for you."

"I still have the photographs," Michael said. "I can still use them. You're not the only one with something to bargain with."

"I hate to tell you this," Smith said. "But they're worthless now. All has been revealed, and nobody gives a fuck. You have two choices."

"Go on."

"You stop with this blackmail crap and find another way to live your life, or you get ready for the shitstorm of all shitstorms that's heading your way. It's up to you. You're a seriously bad blackmailer."

"And that's it?" Michael said. "I get rid of the photos and that's it. You won't be back?"

"I won't be back."

   "Who are you?" Michael said. "Who exactly are you? That ID looked legit."

"I'll see myself out," Smith said. "Don't do anything foolish now."

CHAPTER SEVENTEEN

"How was your day?"

Whitton looked worn out. It was just past six and she was slumped on the chair in the kitchen. Smith had poured her a beer. She looked like she needed something stronger.

"My day was exhausting," she said. "What about you? How was your day?"

"Uneventful," Smith lied.

He sensed Whitton wasn't in the mood to hear about his excursion to Fenton. He'd tell her about it another time.

"Let's order a takeaway," he suggested. "I'm in the mood for pizza."

"You haven't eaten pizza for years," Whitton said.

"That's probably why I feel like one now. The girls won't complain."

"Where are Laura and Lucy?"

"They're around somewhere. Do you feel like talking about the case?"

"Not really," Whitton replied. "It would be nice to put it out of my mind for tonight. What did you do all day? The boss wasn't happy about your little trip to Nunthorpe Road."

"He'll forgive me," Smith said.

After the visit to Michael Teasdale Smith reckoned DI Smyth would owe him a few favours.

Whitton had finished her beer, so Smith got them each another one.

"The psycho neighbour got the teaching assistant job," he said.

"That's great news," Whitton said. "She really wanted that job. And Sheila is not a psycho. She's had a rough time of it."

"What pizza do you feel like?"

"Surprise me," Whitton said. "No anchovies though."

"I'll see if I can find the menu."

Whitton shook her head. "Go and find Lucy. She'll have the app on her phone."

"App?"

"This is 2020, Jason," Whitton said. "Nobody uses printed menus anymore."

The food arrived thirty minutes later. Smith had ordered a varied selection, and he was debating whether to take the last slice of the ham and mushroom pizza on the table in front of him. He decided not to. He was already full, and the looks Theakston and Fred were giving him were making him feel guilty. He tore the pizza slice in half, and it was gone in less than a second.

"I saw that," Whitton said.

"It would have only gone in the bin," Smith said. "I hate cold pizza. I'll take care of the dishes – you go and put your feet up."

"We ate pizza straight out of the boxes," Whitton reminded him.

"Then I'll deposit the boxes in the bin," Smith said. "Dishes done. Do you want another beer?"

"Thanks."

Smith got another two bottles out of the fridge. "I don't know what we'd do without beer – beer solves all of life's problems."

* * *

Marcus Green was hankering for a beer. It was Friday night – he had a wad of cash in his pocket and a few pints at the pub would go down very well right now. He'd been planning on spending a bit of the money at the pub on Church Street but that was before the woman had made him the offer he couldn't refuse. He imagined the cold pint in his hand – the condensation on the glass promising the buzz of the first swig. He could envisage the bitter hop taste on his tongue, and he could feel the gratitude in his stomach as the golden liquid made its way down his throat.

A noise above his head interrupted his reverie. It sounded like footsteps on the wooden floors upstairs. He heard the sound of voices. He recognised one of them – it was the woman who'd brought him here, but the other voices weren't familiar. He followed the sounds as they passed over his head and stopped. Then he heard the slam of a door. Marcus wondered if the woman was talking to the newcomers in the room with the single chair in it. Were they the *others* she'd spoken about?

Everything in the house fell silent again. Marcus got up and went to use the bathroom. When he was finished he flushed the toilet but nothing happened. He removed the lid from the cistern and saw that it was empty. Marcus was no plumber, but he knew the water came in via a pipe and this one didn't appear to be doing what it was supposed to do. He located the correct pipe and jiggled it a bit. The water started to trickle out and then the pressure in the flow returned to normal. Marcus washed his hands and dried them on his jeans. He hadn't noticed that the water pressure from the tap was much weaker now.

The footsteps were back. They stopped by the door at the top of the stairs, the door was opened and three people started to walk down into the cellar. Marcus was waiting for them when they reached the bottom. It was the woman who'd brought him here and two men he didn't recognise. He didn't know the men, but he knew what they were. Both were dressed in the uniform of the streets and the reek that came inside the room with them told its own story. It was the stench of too many nights sleeping on God knows what and the stale, putrid smell of unwashed hair and unbrushed teeth.

"Here we are," the woman gestured with a hand towards the room. "This is Marcus. Marcus this is Steve and Henry – they're going to be staying here for a while."

"Alright," the taller of the men said.

Marcus didn't know if it was Steve or Henry.

"Steve," the woman said to the other man. "Aren't you going to say hello to Marcus."

"Hello, Marcus," he obliged. "Nice place you've got here."

The woman looked like she was going to say something but she didn't.

"I don't suppose you can fetch us some beer?" Marcus asked her.

"I'm afraid that's not allowed."

"Just a couple of six-packs?"

"This will only work if you take it seriously. This has to be done properly. Remember, Mother knows best."

She marched back up the stairs and closed the door behind her.

"We'll sneak out when she's gone," the man called Henry suggested.

The click of the lock on the other side of the door told all of them this wasn't an option.

CHAPTER EIGHTEEN

"What's he doing here?"

Smith had come back inside after smoking a cigarette to find Darren Lewis in the kitchen. The father of Lucy's unborn baby was the last person he expected to see tonight.

"Evening, Mr Smith."

Darren was clearly unfazed.

Smith looked at Lucy. "Well? What's he doing here?"

"We thought we'd watch the speech together as a family," she told him.

"What speech?"

"Boris is going to address the nation," Darren told him.

"Who's Boris?"

"Boris Johnson," Whitton said. "The Prime Minister."

"Oh, him," Smith said.

"Technically," Darren said. "He's your boss, isn't he?"

Smith glared at him in reply.

"He's addressing the nation to keep us updated on the proposed measures to tackle the pandemic," Lucy added. "And it's going to mean huge changes if the rumours are to be believed. There's talk of schools closing and people being made to stay at home."

"That's never going to happen," Smith said.

"Don't you watch the news?" Whitton said.

"Not if I can help it."

"This is serious."

"They've already cancelled all Premiership games for the rest of the season," Darren Lewis informed him.

"Sounds very serious," Smith said.

"This could affect the rest of our lives," Lucy said. "And I wanted Darren to be here to watch it with us. He's part of the family now, and families need to stick together at times like these."

Smith took another beer out of the fridge. "What time is this addressing the nation thing supposed to take place?"

"In thirty minutes," Whitton said. "We need to see what the government has planned. The virus has hit British shores and the experts are warning of high numbers of infections."

"I suppose it can't hurt to listen to what Boris has to say," Smith admitted."

An hour later the Smith household was uncharacteristically quiet. The Prime Minister had given his speech and the four people in Smith's living room were all processing the implications of what he'd said in their own way. Smith and Whitton had made sure Laura didn't watch it. They'd bribed the seven-year-old with a bar of chocolate and told her to go and play on her tablet in her room.

"Do you think he's really going to do what he threatened?" Darren was the first to voice his thoughts.

"He's the big boss," Smith said. "The Prime Minister can do what he wants."

"He talked about closing pubs and restaurants," Whitton said. "Making people stay at home unless they have an essential job. What does he even mean by *essential job*? Surely all jobs are essential to keep the economy going."

"It beats me," Smith said. "I imagine the police will be considered essential."

"I won't be too bothered about not having to go to school," Darren said. "I can play more Xbox."

"I think they'll make sure you still do lessons," Whitton told him. "You'll just have to do them at home."

"That bit about wearing masks and social distancing didn't make any sense," Lucy said. "If this thing is as bad as they say it is, it will be impossible to contain it with such basic measures. They say you can get it by touching something someone with the virus has touched, so how are masks and keeping your distance going to help?"

"It's early days," Whitton reassured her. "I'm sure we'll find out more about the severity of the virus soon."

This was an understatement. In the coming weeks life for the people who inhabited the third planet from the sun was going to change forever. The microscopic virus was set to affect the lives of everybody on earth. A cruise ship in Italy would be the catalyst in Europe. It would be the spark that ignited a fire that refused to be extinguished, and millions of people would be forced to make drastic changes.

The pandemic would spread across the globe and when it did hundreds of thousands of people would be caught in its wave of death. Very few of the measures put in place by the different governments across the world would make any difference, and most of the restrictions wouldn't make logical sense. In certain countries Draconian laws would be put into practice – the armed forces would be brought in to enforce these measures and those failing to comply would face heavy penalties.

The people living in the Smith household were all considering the implications of the impending changes. What would it mean for them? Smith was wondering whether a ban on leaving the house would result in a reduction in crime. He didn't think so. Making it an offence to go outside wouldn't deter a criminal. The threat of a mystery virus wasn't going to make much difference to a murderer hell-bent on killing someone.

Whitton's thoughts turned to her parents. She wondered if the proposed ban on leaving the home would mean she wouldn't be able to visit her mum and dad. She imagined it would. And there was also talk about the elderly being more vulnerable. Older people were more susceptible to catching the virus. Harold and Jane were fit for their age, but it still didn't stop Whitton from worrying.

Lucy was mostly concerned for her unborn baby. She didn't know much about the Covid-19 virus, but she was determined to find out more about it. She needed to find out if pregnant women were more at risk, and if so, what could she do to reduce that risk?

Darren Lewis' main concern was being unable to visit his girlfriend. If the government was going to force people to stay at home, when would he be able to see Lucy? His mind was working overtime. He was devising a plan in his head. There must be some way of bypassing the laws that were about to be implemented. The only solution he could come up with wasn't going to work. He would have to move into the Smith household, and he knew for a fact that Smith wouldn't agree to that in a million years.

CHAPTER NINETEEN

Smith reached out to the bedside table and fumbled for his phone. He'd had a restless night. The Prime Minister's speech was set on repeat inside his head but after an hour or so that had been turned off and something else had kept him awake. There was something in the cellar of number 12 Nunthorpe Road that they'd overlooked. He tried to revisit the dark basement room and he'd retraced his steps in his mind's eye, but nothing came to him. There was something wrong with the scene but no matter how much Smith concentrated nothing occurred to him. What was it they'd missed?

It hit him in the early hours of the morning, and it was thanks to Darren Lewis that it did. He'd managed to drift in and out of slumber, but the cellar kept reappearing in his head. It was in one of these moments between wakefulness and sleep that he realised what they'd overlooked. Often in an investigation the evidence they found at a crime scene wasn't the key – sometimes it wasn't what was present at the scene of a brutal murder that was important, and this instance was no different. The thing that had kept Smith awake for most of the night wasn't connected to what was inside the cellar – it was all about what *wasn't* there when they'd searched it.

In the journal written by the doomed Albanians one of them had talked about a games console. Darren Lewis had expressed his approval of Boris Johnson's proposed closure of schools. Darren had told them he would be able to play more Xbox.

Flamur has already made it clear that he will be monopolizing the Xbox.

That was it. They didn't find the Xbox in the cellar when they were down there. And the only conclusion to draw from its absence would put another perspective on the whole investigation. Somebody went down there.

Somebody was in the cellar after the men had perished. They removed the games console and left again.

The clock on Smith's phone told him it was just before seven. It was an acceptable time to get up. He dressed and went downstairs. He composed a short message to Grant Webber. He wanted to ask the Head of Forensics his opinion on the missing Xbox.

Smith switched on the kettle and Webber replied to his message before it had boiled.

Well spotted. What happened to the TV too?

Smith replied with a single word.

TV?

Webber didn't respond to this. Instead, the intro to Thomas Dolby's *You Blinded me with Science* filled the room.

"Webber," Smith answered it.

"I'm not in the mood for a ping-pong game of messages," the Head of Forensics said.

"What did you mean when you asked what happened to the TV? There wasn't a television in the cellar."

"How did the Albanians play the Xbox?" Webber said.

"Ah," Smith cottoned on. "Whoever went down there took the TV as well. Why do you think that was?"

"I have no idea."

"If you're going to deprive four men of food and water until they die, why bother to return to remove something as innocuous as a games console and a television? It's a bit risky, isn't it?"

"It is," Webber agreed.

Something else occurred to Smith. "Whoever removed the Xbox and the TV did it while the fourth victim was still alive. The one in the room behind the reinforced door."

"About that," Webber said. "The door. We found something interesting there."

"Billy told me it could only be locked from the inside."

"That wasn't always the case," Webber said. "Someone went to a lot of trouble with that door. The lock on the outside was plated and then spot welded. Then the entire surface of the door was repainted. It would have been quite a job."

"Interesting," Smith said. "The owner of the house wasn't exactly telling us the truth. He said everything in the cellar was the previous owner's doing, but he also said she used the hidden room for storage. What would be the point in sealing the lock on the front if that was the case?"

"Your mind is sharp this morning," Webber said. "We need to revisit the cellar, don't we?"

"I assume you're using the royal we?"

"Chicken," Webber told him. "I'll get over there this morning."

With that, he ended the call.

Whitton came in. "Who was that?"

"Webber," Smith told her. "Darren bloody Lewis got me thinking. He said he wouldn't mind the schools closing because he'd get more time to play on his Xbox. The diary the Albanians wrote in mentioned an Xbox but it wasn't there when we checked the cellar. Neither was the television."

"We should have spotted that straight away," Whitton said.

"I still don't know what it means. Why did they come back to retrieve the Xbox and the TV?"

"It might not be important."

"Everything is important in a murder investigation," Smith reminded her. "Until we decide that it isn't."

"It's too early in the day to decipher your riddles. Do you want some coffee?"

"Thanks," Smith said. "I'm just going out for a smoke."

CHAPTER TWENTY

"You're not allowed to smoke in here."

Marcus Green had never smoked in his life. He found the habit repulsive and pointless. It was expensive – his medical training had proved how harmful it was, and he couldn't understand why people would want to pay good money to poison themselves.

"That Mother woman said it was forbidden," the man called Steve said. Marcus had managed to get a bit more information out of him during their first night of co-habitation. His name was Steve Floyd and he was twenty-four. He'd been living on the streets for two years. He'd dropped out of university two weeks before he was due to sit his final exams and his parents had written him off. Marcus could relate to his story.

Steve and Henry had met six months ago. Henry Banks was older by three years and his six years living rough had given him a street-savvy edge Steve hadn't quite achieved.

Harry took a deep drag of the cigarette and exhaled a large cloud of smoke.

"We're not allowed beer," he said. "And I'm fucked if I'm giving up the fags too."

"It's against the rules," Steve reminded him.

"Fuck the rules. She's not the boss of me."

"Do you think she'll be back?" Marcus asked.

"Of course she will," Henry said. "She can't lock us down here without seeing if we're alright."

"What did she tell you?" Marcus said.

"Something about a life changing experiment," Steve replied. "I need a piss."

He walked towards the bathroom cubicle.

"She lost me at five-hundred quid," Henry started to laugh and a mild coughing fit ensued.

"What happened to the bloke?" Marcus said. "When I first met her she was with some weird guy."

"He was there too," Henry said. "Dodgy bloke if you ask me."

"I wonder what this experiment of hers is," Marcus said. "Why pay someone to spend time in a cellar? Did she tell you how long you'd be down here?"

"A week, tops. I've never earned five-hundred quid in a week before, and all we have to do is chill down here. Easy money."

"The toilet is broken," Steve informed them. "It won't flush."

"You have to jiggle the pipe," Marcus told him.

"What pipe?"

"Open the lid on the cistern. Give the inlet pipe a few tugs and the water comes back. There must be some kind of blockage in the pipe. I'll do it."

"Anyone for Xbox?" Henry said.

"There's no Internet down here," Steve said. "And that's the Xbox 1. The games are crap."

"Do you have anything better to do?"

"We could see what's on the box."

"Not going to happen." It was Marcus.

"There's a TV there," Steve pointed to it.

"But it's not connected to anything apart from the Xbox. It was the first thing I checked."

"Great," Steve said. "So, we've got no Internet, no TV and no phones. What the hell sort of experiment is this?"

"Who needs a phone?" Marcus said. "The Mother woman asked me if I had one, and she didn't believe me when I said I hadn't had a phone for two years."

"Well," Steve said. "She took ours. She said we could have them back when this was over."

"She didn't take my phone," Henry said.

"She did. I saw you give it to her."

"That was my spare," Henry said. "I've always had two phones. I gave her the shit one."

He reached inside his pocket and took out an iPhone. It looked brand new.

"Where did you get that?" Steve said.

"You don't want to know," Henry said.

"What good will it do anyway?" Marcus said. "There's no Internet down here."

"No," Henry said. "But there is a weak signal. Especially at the top of the stairs."

"And how is that going to help us?" Steve wondered.

"You can buy mobile data," Marcus suggested.

"I don't have enough credit. But I've got enough to make a few calls."

"Who you gonna call?" Steve said.

"Ghostbusters."

Marcus and Henry said this in unison. A high five followed and they started to laugh.

"This isn't going to be too bad," Henry decided.

"If you say so," Steve said. "I'm already starting to feel claustrophobic."

"Lighten up," Marcus said. "It's a week. We've got loads of food and there are more Xbox games than anyone can get through in seven days. We've got a roof over our heads, and we don't have to put up with the crap on the streets."

"Plus there's five hundred big ones coming our way afterwards," Marcus reminded them.

"And I already know what I'm going to do with it."

"Pub?" Marcus guessed.

"I reckon you and me are going to be good friends."

"I'm glad you're all upbeat about it," Steve said. "I don't know what it is, but I've got a really bad feeling about this place."

CHAPTER TWENTY ONE

"I've got a really bad feeling about this, boss."

Smith was sitting opposite DI Smyth in his office. There was an unlit cigarette in the corner of his mouth.

"You get a bad feeling about every investigation," DI Smyth reminded him. "And you know there's no smoking allowed inside the station."

Smith left the cigarette where it was. "I'm not smoking. I'm trying to cut down and it helps me to think when I've got a cigarette in my mouth."

"Just don't let anyone see you. What's on your mind? And welcome back, by the way."

Smith had been given the green light to return to active duty. Dr Vennell had been true to her word and the process had been very quick.

"Thanks," he said. "I'm starting to wonder if those Albanians were the start of something," Smith said.

"Go on."

"I don't have any further theories," Smith admitted. "The stuff in the journal talks about some kind of experiment devised by this *Mother* woman. What is she hoping to achieve by depriving men of food and water and waiting for them to die? What scientific conclusion is she expecting to get out of this experiment? How long can a human being survive without water? Without food? You can look up that kind of thing on the Internet – you don't have to murder four men to get that information."

"We still don't have enough evidence to conclude that these men were murdered."

"They were murdered, boss," Smith insisted. "That woman might as well have put a gun to their heads and pulled the trigger. She locked them up and waited for them to die. Why?"

DI Smyth sighed and rubbed his eyes. "This is one of those instances where your motive needs to be put on the back burner."

"I don't have one," Smith said. "I've thought long and hard about it, but I can't think of the motivation in this instance."

"Then put it out of your head," DI Smyth said. "And focus on what you know is fact. Four Albanian men were targeted by this woman. Where did she find them? Where did these men come from? And if you say Albania, I'll show you the door."

"I wasn't going to," Smith said. "I'm not DC Moore. But you've got a good point – how did she choose them? If they're illegals we can assume they're not in the system. They probably don't know many people here in the city and that means there aren't many people likely to miss them. That's why she chose them, but we need to ask ourselves how she found them in the first place."

"That's what we focus on then."

"I need to tell you something," Smith said.

"What have you done now?"

"Why do you always assume the worst when I say stuff like that?"

DI Smyth didn't reply to this but the expression on his face told Smith everything he needed to know.

"Fair enough," he said, "I took a trip to Fenton yesterday."

"Never heard of the place," DI Smyth said.

"It's a village on the outskirts of Leeds," Smith said. "And it's where Michael Teasdale lives."

"Am I supposed to know who that is?"

"You met him in Thailand," Smith elaborated. "He must have given you a false name."

"I see. Why do I get the impression I'm not going to like this?"

"You might be surprised," Smith said. "Me and Michael had a friendly chat, and you won't be hearing from him again."

"Did this friendly chat involve the threat of violence?"

"You know me, boss," Smith said. "I'm not a big fan of violence. Let's just say we came to an agreement that benefits everyone concerned. You don't have to cough up fifty grand and Mr Teasdale doesn't get any inconvenient visits from the police or the taxman."

"What about the photographs?"

"Ancient history," Smith said. "They've all been wiped out."

Smith wasn't quite sure if this was true, but he didn't want to share these concerns with DI Smyth.

"How did you find him?" the DI asked.

"Through his mobile phone number," Smith told him. "Michael Teasdale is a terrible blackmailer. He neglected to withhold his number when he sent you the messages. That was a stupid thing to do."

DI Smyth raised an eyebrow. "You had a bit of help."

"Baldwin," Smith admitted. "I wouldn't have been able to find the bastard without her."

"So she knows?"

"She knows, boss," Smith said. "And it's no big deal."

"I don't want this to be common knowledge just yet. I still need some time to think."

"What is there to think about?" Smith asked.

"It's complicated."

"It isn't," Smith disagreed. "I know for a fact that nobody on the team will give two hoots. It won't change a thing."

"I'm not worried about the team, Smith," DI Smyth said. "When this gets out, I have my family to consider. And that's a different kettle of fish altogether. My father is especially old-fashioned."

Smith took a moment to consider this. It didn't take him long.

"If your old man has a problem with it," he said. "Then it's entirely *his* problem. Not yours."

"That's easy to say," DI Smyth said. "But you don't know my father."

"I know if one of my girls came to me with news like this it wouldn't change a thing. We love our kids whatever. That's how it's meant to be."

"You're a good man, Smith," DI Smyth said. "In a slightly delusional way. Your version of the world is clearly different to mine, but I appreciate it. I think it's time we made a start on finding out more about those Albanians."

CHAPTER TWENTY TWO

Smith wasn't going to waste time on hunting down anyone who may have come into contact with the Albanian men. That kind of grunt work didn't appeal to him. Instead, he decided to pay Arthur Miller a visit. There were a few questions Whitton and DI Smyth had neglected to ask him, and Smith needed some answers. The owner of number 12 Nunthorpe Road lived in a house that was in a much better state than the one in Scarcroft. The exterior of the four-bedroom detached Georgian property was immaculate. The house looked onto the green of the Clifton Backies nature reserve. Smith parked his car outside the house and he and DC King got out. A dog barked somewhere in the distance. Smith looked across the road to the entrance of the reserve. He'd never been here before, and he wondered if Theakston and Fred would enjoy the park. It would be a nice change of scenery for them.

"What's it like to be back, Sarge?" DC King asked.

"It's a relief," Smith said. "I dread to think what I'll do when I'm forced to retire for good."

"That's not for a long time."

"Life has a habit of creeping up on you, Kerry."

"Very deep. Did you see the PM's speech?"

"Unfortunately, yes," Smith said. "I wonder what it's going to mean for us."

"I'm sure we'll soon find out. Do you think Mr Miller knows something about what happened to those Albanian men?"

"There's only one way to find out."

Arthur Miller didn't seem surprised to see them. He invited them in and offered them something to drink. Smith declined.

"Is anyone else here?" he asked.

"It's just me," Arthur said.

"Are you not married?" DC King said.

"My wife died. It's been four years now."

"Sorry to hear that."

"She suffered a stroke," Arthur said. "And the underpaid and overworked healthcare workers misdiagnosed it. It was a mild stroke, and she probably would have recovered, but it was left too long and the next one was fatal."

"When you spoke with our colleagues," Smith said. "You mentioned something about the cellar being a part of number 12 Nunthorpe Road when you bought it."

"That's correct," Arthur said. "I gave the detectives the details of the previous owner."

"You also said she used the room next to the cellar for storage. Is that right?"

"I think so."

"Did you go down to the cellar much?" DC King said.

"I didn't go inside the house very often," Arthur said.

"Why is that?" Smith said.

"There's no need. I own four properties and most of the time they're let out to tenants."

"But the house in Scarcroft wasn't," DC King said.

"I was in the process of fixing it up," Arthur said. "I did mention this to the other officers."

"What exactly did this fixing up entail?" Smith said. "When I was there, it didn't appear that much work was going on."

"I've been busy. I was planning on giving the interior walls a lick of paint. The previous tenants left the place in a bit of a state, and it was deemed unfit for habitation."

"Who decided that?" DC King said.

"The council of course. The majority of my tenants are on benefits, but the council check to see if the properties meet the standards as per the guidelines set out by God knows who. It's a joke. If they did a better job of vetting potential tenants, the property wouldn't have been in such a state in the first place."

"Who was last in the house?" Smith asked.

"God knows," Arthur replied.

"You don't keep a record?" DC King said. "You don't know who's living in your houses? What about a damage deposit? I thought that was common practice."

"You'll have to ask the council about that."

"We're going to need a list of all past tenants," Smith said. "Everyone who has lived in the house in Scarcroft."

"Again, you'll have to get that from the council. They put the tenants in there. I get my rent, and that's all I can say."

"And everyone's happy," Smith added.

"Excuse me?"

"Nothing. I assume you have a contact at the council?"

"I'd have to dig it out."

"We'd appreciate it if you could," DC King said.

"Can you tell us why the water and electricity was disconnected at 12 Nunthorpe Road?" Smith said.

"I didn't realise it was," Arthur said. "The accounts are up to date."

"Someone turned them off manually. Was that your doing?"

"I don't know anything about it. I certainly didn't do it. What reason would there be for me to turn off the water and electricity?"

"Let's get back to the cellar," Smith said. "Did you ever rent that part of the house out?"

"Once or twice," Arthur said. "But most of the time it's not used."

"So it's off limits to the tenants?"

"That's correct."

"When you were down there last," Smith said. "Did you notice anything odd about the reinforced door?"

"Odd?"

"The lock on the front had been rendered unusable," Smith elaborated. "It was modified in such a way that it could only be locked from the inside. Do you have any idea why someone would do that?"

"It beats me," Arthur said. "The only possible reason someone would do that would be to create a kind of panic room."

"A panic room?" DC King repeated.

"You know, when someone breaks into the house, you've..."

"My colleague knows what a panic room is, Mr Miller," Smith interrupted. "But this didn't look like any panic room I've ever seen. There was no food or water stored in there – no electricity, and no possible means of contacting anyone to raise the alarm."

"I really can't help you," Arthur said.

"You told us you heard rumours about squatters in the house," Smith changed tack.

"I overheard Mrs Pratt mentioning it to Ali at the corner shop," Arthur said.

"And Mrs Pratt didn't think to contact you directly about it?" DC King said.

"We've never really got on."

"Why is that?" Smith asked.

"She blames me for the rubbish the council place in the house. It's not my decision who gets placed in my houses. I don't get to choose my tenants, but Mrs Pratt still blames me."

"What kind of *rubbish* are we talking about?" Smith said.

"All sorts. You know, unemployed wasters, single mothers, immigrants. Although the immigrants are much better behaved than the English the council stick in there."

"Have you had problems with squatters in the past?" Smith said.

"On and off," Arthur said. "The houses are secure but those kind of people will always find a way in."

"Desperate people?" DC King said. "People with nowhere to live?"

"Don't come with your namby pamby, politically correct guff, young lady. I've heard all the sob stories. You'd soon change your tune if it was your house they were living in for nowt. And it's almost impossible to get them out. That's how great this country is nowadays."

"We won't keep you for much longer."

Smith didn't feel like getting into this kind of discussion.

"I assume your fingerprints were taken when you were questioned at the station."

"It's bloody outrageous," Arthur said. "I'm the victim in this and I'm the one treated like a common criminal."

"I'll take that as a yes then," Smith decided. "And believe me you weren't the victim in this. Not even close. We'll need those contact details we spoke about."

"When will I be able to get my house back?"

"When we get the answers we need," Smith told him. "And not before then."

CHAPTER TWENTY THREE

"It stinks in here."

Steve Floyd was pacing up and down. The cellar was uncomfortably warm, and he was dressed in only a T-Shirt and a pair of boxer shorts.

"It's ever since you took off your jeans," Henry told him. "When was the last time you changed your underpants?"

"It's not me," Steve said. "It's something else."

"There are no windows down here," Marcus said. "There's very little air circulation. We're breathing in stale air and there will be a much greater concentration of carbon dioxide. The air we exhale will be a few degrees warmer than normal because of the respiration process being hindered by the extra CO2."

"What are you," Steve said. "A scientist?"

"A doctor," Marcus said, and qualified it with: "Almost. I quit the medical degree in the final year."

"That's good to know," Henry said. "At least if one of us gets ill we've got a doctor in the house. Who wants to go next? Who wants to get their arse kicked?"

He held up the game controller.

"I hate zombie blasting games," Steve said.

"You need to lighten up, mate. You've been a miserable bastard ever since you came down here."

"I wonder why," Steve said. "We've been locked in a cellar. We don't know if that *Mother* woman is even coming back. There's no TV and no Internet and all the Xbox games are shit. There are no windows, and the doc here tells us we're probably going to suffocate down here, so I wonder why I'm feeling a bit edgy."

"We're not going to suffocate," Henry said. "Tell him, doc."

"We won't run out of air," Marcus obliged. "It's stuffy down here but the place isn't totally sealed. There's still plenty of air coming in from the gap under the door and the vents in the walls. Try taking a few deep breaths – it'll help."

"I need a shit," Steve informed them.

"That ought to improve the stench in here," Henry said.

Steve glared at him but kept quiet.

"How long do you think it'll be before she comes back?" Henry asked Marcus.

"She told us we'd be down here for a week," Marcus said. "It's possible we won't see her again before then."

"Steve is starting to get on my tits," Henry whispered.

"He needs to try and relax," Marcus whispered back. "Accept that this is where we're going to spend the next six days and get on with it. It'll pass in no time."

"We're supposed to write in the journal," Henry said. "That was part of the deal. I'm hopeless at writing."

"I'll do it," Marcus offered. "It'll give me something to do. Maybe it'll make me famous one day."

"It can be the cellar experiment. It's got a good ring to it. Kind of like the Blair Witch Project."

"The cellar experiment," Marcus repeated. "I'm going to write that on the front of the journal. I like it – The Cellar Experiment."

* * *

Heidi London was a frumpy woman in her mid-fifties. The brown hair on her head was clearly not her own. The wig was ill fitted and she'd adjusted it three times before she even invited Smith and DC King inside the house. Arthur Miller had given Smith the details of the previous owner of 12

Nunthorpe Road and Heidi had been more than happy to speak to them when he called.

Heidi led them to a small, tidy living room and told them to take a seat. "Can I get you something to drink?"

"Coffee would be great," Smith said.

"I'll pop the kettle on."

"What's this all about?" she asked when she came back with a tray of coffee, milk and sugar.

"A house you once owned," Smith said.

He poured himself a cup of coffee and added two sugars.

"The house on Nunthorpe Road?" Heidi said.

"That's right. You sold the place to Arthur Miller a couple of years ago. Is that right?"

"Is it only a couple of years?" Heidi said. "It feels like longer. What's he been saying about me?"

"Sorry?"

"Miller. What's he saying I've done now?"

"Have you had problems with Mr Miller?" DC King asked.

"For the first six months he never left me alone," Heidi said. "This isn't working – this needs fixing. He viewed the place, must be over a dozen times before he put in an offer. He knew what he was buying."

"What kind of things did he complain about?" Smith said.

"Anything he could think of. What's this all about? Why has he sent the police round here?"

"He didn't," Smith told her. "We're here to talk about the cellar in the house."

"Go on."

"Did you build the cellar yourself?"

"Good Lord no," Heidi said. "But I must admit it was one of the selling points. I have two kids. Two boys. They're grown up now but when they were teenagers, they were quite a handful. The cellar was somewhere they could go to let off a bit of steam. Somewhere they could call their own. You know what teenagers are like."

"I certainly do," Smith said.

The doorbell rang and Heidi got up to see who it was. She returned shortly afterwards.

"Sorry about that. Amazon delivery. Where were we?"

"You were telling us about the cellar," DC King said.

"Can you explain why it was soundproofed?" Smith asked.

"That was Barry's suggestion," Heidi said. "He's my eldest, and he liked to invite his band down there to practice. I told him the neighbours would complain, but the drummer in the band said he could soundproof the place for me. Didn't even charge me for it, and he did a great job."

"There's another room down there," Smith said. "What was that room used for?"

"I used it for storage," Heidi said. "Stuff I didn't use very often, but I still wanted to keep."

"The door is a bit excessive, isn't it?" DC King said. "Why did you need a steel, reinforced door?"

"It was already there when I bought the place."

"When exactly was that?" Smith said.

"Just after Barry was born. Norman and I realised we needed a bigger place and the house on Nunthorpe Road was going for a song."

"How old is Barry?" DC King said.

"Thirty-two."

"Norman is your husband?" Smith said.

"That's right. He's over in Barmston right now, doing some work on the cottage."

"Cottage?" DC King said.

"It's a little seaside holiday place we bought."

Smith wasn't sure what else to ask her. He decided to bring up the modified lock on the front of the reinforced door.

"When you lived at Nunthorpe Road," he said. "Did the reinforced door in the cellar have a lock on it?"

"It did," Heidi confirmed.

"On the front?" DC King added.

Heidi frowned. "Where else would the lock be?"

Smith didn't think there was anything left to discuss. He thanked Heidi for the coffee and got to his feet.

"Why are you so interested in my old house?" Heidi said.

"I'm afraid I can't discuss that," Smith informed her. "Thank you for your time."

CHAPTER TWENTY FOUR

"All the water's finished."

Henry was standing in front of the fridge. The door was wide open and he was staring inside.

"Close the fridge door," Steve told him. "You're going to let all the cold air out."

"There isn't much food left in there anyway."

"I thought we had more water than that," Marcus said.

"So did I," Henry said. "There were at least six two-litre bottles in there yesterday evening."

"I used four of them to fill up the bath a bit," Steve informed them.

"You did what?" Marcus said.

"There wasn't any water coming from the tap," Steve said. "And I needed a bath. You keep telling me I stink."

"So you used up our drinking water?" Henry said.

"I thought we could just fill up the bottles from the tap," Steve said. "But there's nothing coming out of any of the taps anymore."

"You fucking idiot." It was Marcus.

"It's not my fault the taps are dry."

"They were working fine yesterday," Marcus said.

"What did you do to them?" Henry asked Steve.

Steve held up his hands. "Don't look at me – the water just stopped. Do you have the number for that woman?"

"No. I'm not supposed to have a phone remember."

"What about you?" Steve looked at Marcus.

"I don't own a phone. Why would I take down someone's number?"

"Fuck," Steve said. "What are we going to do now?"

"I'll take a look at the taps," Marcus offered. "It's probably something simple."

It wasn't. After half-an-hour of fiddling Marcus admitted defeat. No matter what he did to the taps, nothing worked. They had no running water. He broke the news to his roommates.

"What do we do now?" Henry asked.

"How long can we last without water?" Steve said.

"Three days, tops," Marcus informed them. "Is there no water anywhere?" Harry nodded to the two-litre bottle on the small table in the middle of the room. There was about three inches of water in the bottom.

"That's all we have."

"This isn't good," Marcus stated the obvious. "We need to find a way out of here."

"She locked the door," Steve reminded him.

"And that's the only exit," Henry added. "It's the only way in and out of the cellar."

"Does anyone have any suggestions?" Steve said.

"We start screaming," Marcus said. "We scream as loud as we can and hope someone hears us."

A man walking past the house with his dog was aware of a muffled noise coming from somewhere close by – the ears of the Labrador pricked up, but they carried on walking. Both man and dog were blissfully unaware that three homeless men were screaming their lungs out in the cellar of number 29 Norton Road.

* * *

"Four Albanian men are dead," DI Smyth said. "And nobody is missing them."

As opening statements went this wasn't the most inspirational one the team had heard at a briefing.

"Ardit, Busar, Erjon and Flamur are common Albanian names apparently, but nobody with those names has been reported missing."

"We expected as much," Smith said. "Probably half of the Albanians in the city aren't registered anywhere. That's why these men were chosen. They were selected for that specific reason. It's much easier to get away with killing someone who isn't in the system."

"The cause of death for all four men has been confirmed as severe dehydration," DI Smyth continued. "The wounds inflicted on three of the men were definitely bite marks. Dr Bean is ninety-five percent certain the man in the hidden room was responsible for these wounds. He found the remains of what appears to be human flesh in the stomach of that man. I'm sure you'll all agree that we don't need to spend any more time dwelling on that aspect of the murders."

"I'm happy with that," DC Moore said.

"Same here," Bridge seconded.

"I wonder what made him do that." It was Smith.

He was curious.

"What could possibly drive a man to eat the flesh of his friends?"

"I thought we weren't going to go into that?" Whitton said.

"He must have been desperate to do that. I can't imagine what must have been going through his head at the time."

"Moving on," DI Smyth cut short Smith's musings. "What did we get from the previous owner of the house?"

"Not much," Smith told him. "Heidi London bought 12 Nunthorpe Road thirty-odd years ago. The cellar was already there, as was the room with the metal door."

"She said the door could be locked from the outside," DC King added.

"Which means the outer lock was blocked off after she sold the house."

"Arthur Miller reckons the door was intact too," Smith said. "But he also told us he hadn't been down in the cellar for a while. It looks like whoever locked those men down there did that to the front of the door."

"Why?" Bridge wondered. "Why did they do that?"

"To enable you to get away from flesh eaters," DC Moore speculated.

"The man found in that room was the flesh eater, Harry," Smith reminded him.

"That's enough," DI Smyth said. "That topic of conversation is over."

"The power and water were cut off manually," Smith said. "Arthur Miller said it was nothing to do with him."

"Do you think he was telling the truth?" Whitton asked.

"I got the impression he was. It's looking likely that the person who locked those men down there is the same one who cut the power and the water supply. The electricity was on to begin with. The author of the journal talked about playing Xbox, so there must have been power."

"The journal made for disturbing reading," DI Smyth said. "But even if we read between the lines, it doesn't really give us much information about the woman who imprisoned the four men."

"Mother," Smith said. "Why did they call her that?"

"She's hardly a mother figure," Whitton said. "What kind of mother locks someone up and waits for them to die?"

"Why didn't she take the journal?" Smith said out of the blue.

"What are you thinking?" DI Smyth said.

"We know someone came back for the Xbox and the TV," Smith said. "Why didn't they take the journal too? If this really is some kind of sick experiment, surely that journal would be important."

"Smith's right," DC King said. "Why did they leave the journal behind?"

Baldwin came inside the room before anyone had a chance to put forward any theories on that.

"Sorry to interrupt, but a call just came in from a man called Henry Banks."

"Who's he?" Bridge asked.

"I didn't get the chance to ask him, Sarge," Baldwin said. "The phone line was terrible, but I did manage to get the gist of the phone call before the line went dead. This Henry Banks claimed he and two other men were being held against their will somewhere in Murton."

"Did he sound genuine?" Smith said.

"He did, Sarge," Baldwin confirmed. "He seemed terrified."

"Did he give you an address?" DI Smyth said.

"He didn't know, sir. He just said it was somewhere in Murton."

"Murton Park isn't very built up," Bridge remembered.

"Didn't he give you any idea of where in Murton he was being held captive?" DI Smyth asked.

"He really couldn't tell me," Baldwin said. "But he did tell me this: Henry has been living on the streets for years, and now he and two other homeless men are locked in a cellar."

CHAPTER TWENTY FIVE

"I know him."

The man standing in front of Smith could benefit from a visit to the dentist. His smile revealed a row of brown teeth and the stench that accompanied his words caused Smith to take a step back. It had taken him two hours - a lot of frustrating dead ends and forty pounds of DC King's money to get the answers he wanted. The man with the halitosis seemed genuine and a spark of recognition had appeared in his eyes as soon as Smith mentioned Henry Banks's name. He'd introduced himself as George.

"When was the last time you saw Henry?" DC King asked.

"Probably yesterday," George said.

"Do you know him well?" Smith said.

"As well as you know anyone on the streets. He was a laugh. We'd sometimes hook up and chat."

"Can you describe him?" DC King said.

"Tall," George told her. "At least six-three. Brown hair and blue eyes I think. He has a big nose."

"What time did you see him yesterday?" Smith said.

"Early. Probably around eight in the morning."

"And you haven't seen him since that?"

"Can't say I have," George said. "He usually parks off on the square round the corner from the Minister on Saturdays. Him and another bloke."

"Do you know this other bloke?" Smith said.

"Steve his name is. Weird guy."

"And you haven't seen him since yesterday?" DC King said.

"What's he done?"

"We're just trying to find him," Smith said. "We need his help."

"I have to go," George said. "The afternoon drinkers will be out of the pubs soon. The booze makes them generous."

Smith handed him one of his cards. "If you see Henry again, please give me a call."

George took the card, glanced at it and sighed. "With what?"

"Excuse me?" Smith said.

"Airtime isn't free."

"Of course," Smith turned to DC King.

She shook her head and took out a ten-pound note. She handed the money to George. The homeless man snatched it away and bowed his head.

"Much obliged. I'll keep my eyes open."

    "I think I met Henry Banks yesterday, Kerry," Smith told DC King when George had gone.

"It didn't occur to me until just now," Smith added. "There was a homeless man by the car park in Monk Bar. It was just after my appointment with the psychiatrist. He told me his name was Henry and he matched the description our mate George gave us. Tall, brown hair, big nose. I gave him a few cigarettes. I didn't have any cash on me."

"About that, Sarge," DC King said. "This hunting expedition has cost me fifty quid."

"I'll pay you back."

    Smith looked up and down the street. It was mid-afternoon and Gillygate was packed with people. Locals and tourists alike were making the most of the Saturday warm weather. The shops and pubs were doing a roaring trade. Something occurred to Smith.

"Come on, Kerry," he said.

"Where are we going?"

"Monk Bar car park."

"But your car is parked in Bootham Row."

"The man who I believe is Henry Banks bummed the smokes off me in the

Monk Bar car park," Smith told her. "And what do all public car parks have in common?"

"CCTV?" DC King guessed.

They passed more homeless people as they walked. Smith wondered if these lost souls had always been here and he realised he hadn't really paid them much attention before.

"Where do all these people come from, Kerry?"

"It's getting to be a nationwide problem," DC King said. "There are more and more homeless people these days than ever before."

"I thought there were shelters for them."

"Space is limited, and a lot of these people don't have any ID. To get a place in a shelter you need to register and that requires some form of identification. It's very sad."

"Don't these people have families who can help them?" Smith asked.

"A lot of them are in this situation because of their families. It's the same in Bradford – it's the same all over. I wonder what will happen when the pandemic restrictions come into effect. Where are these people going to go?"

"Nothing has been set in stone yet."

"It will be," DC King said. "People are going to be forced to stay at home, but how is that possible when you don't even have a home to call your own?"

Smith found what he was looking for as soon as they reached the Monk Bar car park. There were two cameras – one on either side of the car park.

"We need to find out where the footage is stored," Smith said.

"It will be with the car park operator," DC King told him. "I'll ask Baldwin to get hold of the local authority to request access. What time did you speak to Henry Banks yesterday?"

"The appointment with Dr Vennell finished just after eleven. So ask for the footage between eleven and half past."

"I'll ask Baldwin to request the footage from both cameras," DC King said and took out her phone.

Five minutes later they'd got the ball rolling. Baldwin promised to make it a priority and she reckoned they should have the CCTV footage within the hour.

"What are we going to do with the camera footage?" DC King asked Smith.

"Circulate a photo of George Banks," Smith said. "Ask the public for any information about him. Someone might have seen him with the woman who locked him in the cellar."

"We still don't know if it was the same woman. We can't be certain it was the *Mother* woman the Albanians wrote about in the journal."

"How many people have you come across who've been locked in a cellar during the course of your career, Kerry?"

"Only one."

Smith frowned.

"I'm looking at him, Sarge," DC King explained.

"I'm trying to forget about that," Smith said.

"I suppose it is suspicious."

"The phone call from Henry Banks is connected to those dead Albanians," Smith insisted. "I just wish we'd got more information from him before the line went dead."

CHAPTER TWENTY SIX

"That's just great."

Steve Floyd was glaring at Henry Banks.

"The one phone call that could mean life or death to us and your phone battery dies."

"I didn't realise it was low," Henry said.

"Perhaps you ought to have checked something like that."

"Because I knew we'd end up locked in a fucking cellar, didn't I? With no water and no electricity. If you hadn't decided to use all of the drinking water to clean your balls, we wouldn't be in this mess. We could have made it last a week."

"Calm down." It was Marcus. "It's still possible someone will find us. You told the police officer we were somewhere in Murton. There aren't many residential properties here, and very few of them will have cellars."

"How are the police even going to check?" Steve said. "Do you think they're going to knock on all the doors and ask the owners if they have a cellar in the house? In case you've forgotten, we're the only ones here. They're not going to find us."

"Your optimism is outstanding," Henry commented. "They can check the plans of the buildings. A cellar has to be on the plans and they can get that from the Deeds Office."

"You could just do the obvious thing," Marcus said. "And charge the phone. I assume you have a charger."

Henry grinned and walked over to his bag. He unzipped it and removed the charger, complete with adaptor.

"What was that noise?" Steve asked and looked at the ceiling.

"I didn't hear anything," Henry said.

"There," Steve pointed to the corner of the ceiling. "It sounds like someone's up there."

"I heard it too," Marcus said.

"Perhaps Mother has come back," Steve suggested.

They could hear the sound of voices now. It wasn't clear what was being said but it sounded like there were at least two of them.

"It could be the cops," Marcus said.

He was up the stairs in a flash. He reached the door and started to bang his hands against it.

"We're down here."

The voices stopped, and everything upstairs was still.

"Down here," Marcus screamed. "We're down in the cellar."

He looked down into the room. Steve was gazing up at him. Henry was attaching the charger to his phone. Marcus watched as he located the plug socket and inserted the adapter into it.

The lights went out and everything turned black.

* * *

"I want this face staring at everyone in the city before this evening."

Smith was sitting opposite PC Neil Walker inside the press liaison officer's office. On the table in front of PC Walker was a close-up photo of the man they believed to be Henry Banks.

"We have reason to believe he's been locked in a cellar somewhere in Murton," Smith added. "Together with two other men."

The rest of the team were sifting through the housing plans for all the residential properties in Murton. There were more of them than they initially thought, and it was clear it was going to be an exhausting task.

"We also believe the person who imprisoned them in the cellar is the same woman who was responsible for the deaths of the four Albanians," Smith said.

"About that," PC Walker said. "We're getting a bit of backlash in the press about that."

"What kind of backlash?"

"The usual," PC Walker said. "The usual guff about police nonchalance due to who the men were."

"That's nonsense. We're doing everything we can. I don't give a shit where a murder victim comes from – they could be from Timbuktu or they could be from the city, I treat them all the same."

"It'll blow over," PC Walker said. "But you might want to prepare yourself for flak from top brass. When illegals are murdered it becomes political."

"Bollocks. It's not political. How soon can we have that photo out there?"

"Give me an hour. What's going on?"

"I really don't know," Smith said. "It looks like someone is preying on vulnerable people – street people, and these people are not getting what they were promised. The Albanians were told they would get food, water and a roof over their heads and a few hundred quid on top of that, but what they got was a long, drawn-out death."

"Good God. Why do that? What do they get out of it?"

"It's looking like it's some kind of twisted experiment," Smith said. "But I still haven't figured out the aim of the experiment. Can I leave the photo in your hands?"

"No problem."

Smith left the office and headed up to the canteen. He needed some strong coffee. He selected the strongest the machine had to offer and took a seat by the window. His phone started to ring the moment he sat down. The screen told him it was a number that wasn't in his contact's list.

"Smith," he answered it.

"Can you talk?" a familiar voice asked.

"Who is this?"

"Dr Vennell. We had an appointment yesterday."

"I haven't forgotten already," Smith said. "Thanks for speeding things up. I appreciate it."

"I was wondering if you were free this evening."

Smith wasn't expecting this.

"Are you still there?" Dr Vennell said.

"I'm still here," Smith said. "What did you have in mind?"

"I'd like to pick your brains. I'd very much like to discuss an old case with you. We can always make it another time."

Smith thought for a second. It was Saturday and as far as he was aware, he and Whitton hadn't made any plans.

"Which case are you interested in?" he asked.

"A very curious one," Dr Vennell said. "The police murders."

Smith remembered it well.

"The Ghosts investigation? Why are you so interested in that one?"

"We can discuss that when we meet."

"Do you want me to come to you?"

"Let's make it a neutral location," Dr Vennell said. "You choose."

It didn't take Smith long to decide. He told Dr Vennell where he had in mind, and they agreed to meet at eight.

CHAPTER TWENTY SEVEN

"According to the records we got from the Deeds Office, six properties in the Murton area have basement rooms."

DI Smyth wrote the addresses on the whiteboard in the small conference room.

"How up to date are the plans?" Smith asked.

"They're up to date," DI Smyth said. "Whenever a homeowner wants to do extensive renovations to a property they have to go through the relevant channels. Planning permission needs to be granted, and the subsequent building work is updated on the plans."

"People still do work without getting permission," Bridge pointed out. "My old neighbour built an extension that blocked out half the light in our living room, and when my old man complained to the council it turned out the neighbour hadn't got permission. He had to knock the whole lot down."

"It is possible that a cellar was built without the proper permission," DI Smyth agreed. "But it's highly unlikely. Building a cellar is a major job. It would be impossible to undertake such a job on the sly."

"What's the plan of action?" Smith said.

"I've sent a couple of uniform out to Murton," DI Smyth said.

"A couple of uniform? We need to take this seriously."

"As of now, we can't justify any more than that. We still don't know exactly how this Henry Banks fits into the equation, and until we have more information at our disposal that's as much as we can do. The budget is tight as it is, and resources have to be used wisely."

"What a crock of shit," Smith said.

"Excuse me?"

"According to PC Walker we're getting flak for not taking the murders of the Albanians seriously. The press liaison officer warned me that top brass are probably going to make this political, and you're talking about resources. The men and women wearing the pips will want this to go away – as far as I can see we can exploit as many resources as we see fit."

"What are you suggesting?"

"I'm saying we should be making a noise in Murton," Smith said. "Instead of wasting time discussing what we can and cannot afford to use resources on. There are three men imprisoned in a cellar somewhere in Murton and all three are going to die if we don't find them."

"We don't know that for sure," DC Moore dared.

"The man who phoned needs to be taken seriously."

"We are taking it seriously," DI Smyth said. "If those men are in a cellar in Murton uniform will find them. We have other matters to discuss."

Smith folded his arms and waited for DI Smyth to continue.

"Let's run through the series of events from the beginning," he said. "On Thursday Arthur Miller phoned us after discovering three dead men in the cellar of the house he owns in Nunthorpe Road. Mr Miller was alerted to possible squatters in his property, and he went in mob-handed to try and get them to leave. He called it in straight away. We now know the men were Albanian and there was a fourth man in the room behind the metal door. According to Mr Miller it had been a while since he was inside the property and even longer since he set foot in the cellar. We've spoken to the previous owner of the house and according to her the cellar was there when she bought the property over thirty years ago. This was confirmed from the plans on the original build of the house."

"Are we disregarding Mr Miller as a suspect?" DC King asked.

"He's still a suspect," Smith decided. "He is the only person with keys to the house. He knows the place inside out, and he had every opportunity to get those men there and lock them in the cellar."

"He was the one who called us about the bodies," DC Moore reminded him.

"And that was a bit too convenient for my liking. He hasn't been in the house for weeks and when he does eventually go inside, he finds three dead men and a man who later died in hospital. Arthur Miller is still right at the top of the list."

"I don't think he was involved," Whitton argued. "I think he was telling us the truth."

"And you're forgetting what was written in the journal," DC King joined in. "The Albanians mentioned someone who called herself Mother. They were tricked by a woman."

"They could be in it together," Smith said. "It's far too early to cross Arthur Miller off the list."

"He's still on the list," DI Smyth said. "And we will be keeping an eye on him, but you seem to be forgetting one thing. If the man who called in earlier was imprisoned by the same person who let the Albanians die it means he would have to gain access to the property in Murton. Mr Miller doesn't own any property in Murton."

"The photograph of the man we believe to be Henry Banks will be distributed soon," Smith changed the subject. "Hopefully someone will know who he is, and it's possible somebody will have seen him with the mysterious *Mother* woman."

"Can I make a suggestion?" DC Moore said.

"Go on, Harry," DI Smyth said.

"Why don't we put some feelers out within the homeless community?"

"Do you realise how ridiculous that sounds?" It was Bridge.

"It's a good suggestion," DI Smyth argued.

"I'm not talking about the suggestion," Bridge said. "It's the term Harry used. *Homeless community*. It's an oxymoron – a contradiction in terms. The very fact that these people are homeless suggests a lack of community, and..."

"Enough," DI Smyth cut Bridge short. "We're wasting time."

His phone started to ring. The conversation was brief and the loud sigh he exhaled when he'd finished told the team it wasn't good news.

"That was PC Black. He and PC Miller have finished in Murton and they came up empty handed. They didn't find anything untoward in any of the cellars in Murton."

"What now then?" Bridge wondered.

The ensuing silence told him nobody had any ideas.

"What about the call log," DC King suggested a few seconds later. "Can't we trace the phone that Henry Banks called from?"

"Only if it's switched on," DC Moore told her. "And even then we'll only get a rough area. Triangulation of the cell masts isn't very accurate."

"It's worth a shot," DI Smyth decided. "Let's just hope Henry Banks still has his phone switched on."

CHAPTER TWENTY EIGHT

"They're not as resilient as the Albanians."
The screen of the laptop had turned black and only the muffled sounds of the men's voices could be heard.
"I thought you said these cameras were the best."
The woman who called herself *Mother* tapped the keypad and a vague greyscale image appeared.
"The man in the shop said they were top of the range. The batteries are supposed to last seven days."
"We're going to need better ones for next time. How long do you think they've got?"
"They're weak," Mother said. "But they're typical of the English these days. The majority of the population aren't going to stand a chance when the plague comes their way. I'll wager that all three of them will be dead by Monday."
"They're scared," Mother's companion stated the obvious.
The face mask had slipped down again. It was promptly readjusted so it covered the mouth and the nose.
"I don't know why you feel the need to keep that thing on inside the house," Mother said. "There's nothing sinister in here."
"It's necessary. The experts are recommending that everyone cover their nose and mouth. This will be mandatory soon, just you wait. People are going to have to rethink their priorities when the virus strikes."
"That's why we're conducting the experiments, remember. We will make a difference."
"They're definitely scared," her friend said and adjusted the mask again.
The voice coming over the speaker was Steve Floyd's. He was telling his roommates they were all going to die.

"How do these people even survive on the streets?" Mother wondered. "This country has gone soft."

"Do you think the police will find them in time?"

"No," Mother said. "They don't even know where to start looking."

"I thought you took their phones."

"So did I. I wasn't to know the tall one had two. It's all one – the phone is as dead as they are. We need to start hunting for the next lab rats. The learning curve is on the up but we're running out of time."

"I suggest we choose some stronger ones next."

"We will," Mother agreed. "The Albanians impressed me, but if this experiment is going to work, it has to be done scientifically. We need a broader spectrum of test cases. I think it's time to introduce the female of the species to the delights of the cellar, and after that I suggest we think about taking some teenagers."

* * *

"Take a seat," Chalmers said.

DI Smyth sat down.

"Before I begin," Chalmers added. "I want to make it clear that this is not me talking. I'm just the messenger."

"Sir," DI Smyth said.

"The CC has expressed concerns," Chalmers carried on. "Those concerns have been passed down to the Super - he subsequently dropped them into my lap, and now I'm giving you a heads-up."

"You're talking about the Albanians."

"I am. Where are we at with that? Because the Chief wants to know when this will be put to bed."

"We're doing everything we can," DI Smyth said. "A call came in a short while ago from a man claiming to have been locked in a cellar. Unfortunately, the line went dead before Baldwin could get the address of the house, but the caller did tell her it was somewhere in Murton."

"And?"

"According to the records at the Deeds Office," DI Smyth said. "Only six properties in Murton have cellars. Uniform were sent out, but there was no sign of the men."

Chalmers stood up and walked over to the window. The sun was low in the sky – it would be dark soon.

"What else do we know?" he asked.

"Smith thinks he met the homeless man yesterday, sir. At the car park in Monk Bar. We requested the CCTV footage from the car park, and we managed to get a decent photo of the man. PC Walker has promised to have it circulated before the end of the day. We'll be asking the public to come forward with any information about Henry Banks. We might get lucky - someone might have seen him talking to the woman who locked him in the cellar."

"Woman?"

"The Albanians wrote in a journal," DI Smyth explained. "And in it they mentioned someone called *Mother*. Smith believes it has to be the same woman who locked the three homeless men up in Murton."

"If Smith thinks that, then I'm inclined to go with it. What else do we have?"

"We're still struggling with a motive. It's becoming clear that it's all part of some sick experiment, but we still haven't figured out the reason for the experiment. We need more time."

"Time is something we don't have. How thoroughly did uniform check the houses in Murton?"

"As thoroughly as two officers could," DI Smyth said. "You know how it goes – the budget is tighter than ever, and resources need to be used wisely."

"Use them as you see fit, Oliver."

"Can I quote you on that, sir?"

"Quote me all you like," Chalmers said. "As I said, the CC wants this to go away. We need to find out what happened to those illegals, and we need to do that yesterday."

"What about the other three men?"

"If they were imprisoned by the same woman," Chalmers said. "It's all one and the same. You say the men are somewhere in Murton?"

"That's what the man called Henry said."

"There aren't many residential properties in that part of town."

"And, according to the building plans, only six have cellars," DI Smyth said.

"Find those men. Is there anything else you're looking into?"

"We're running out of ideas," DI Smyth said. "Hopefully the public appeal will reap rewards, but apart from that we've got very little to go on."

Chalmers sat back down.

"The Super is itching for a press conference."

"We don't have anything to give the general public at this stage," DI Smyth said. "The appeal is going to have to be enough for now."

"What do you think this is about? What's your gut telling you?"

"I'm inclined to agree with Smith," DI Smyth said. "From what was in the journal, it's some kind of experiment. Perhaps it's a test to see how long someone can survive under extreme conditions, but it still doesn't make any logical sense. Unless we're dealing with a twisted sadist, none of us can figure out what the person responsible stands to gain. We didn't find any hidden cameras in the cellar in Scarcroft, so how does this *Mother* woman even know what's happening down there? She came back for the Xbox and the TV but she left the journal. Why leave it behind?"

"Perhaps she wanted us to find it."

"Why?" DI Smyth asked.

Chalmers didn't have an answer to this. "Keep at it. How is Smith bearing up?"

"Smith's the same as always."

"His near-death experience hasn't affected the way his brain works?" Chalmers said.

DI Smyth smiled. "Unfortunately not, sir."

"You can't win 'em all. I'll give the Chief an update. Tell him we're close to cracking this one."

"We're nowhere near."

"The CC doesn't need to know that," Chalmers said. "Keep me in the loop."

CHAPTER TWENTY NINE

Smith was starting to get a headache. The dull pain was making its way from his eyes upwards to his forehead. He found some painkillers in his desk drawer and popped two in his mouth, slowly letting them dissolve under his tongue.

He'd been staring at the screen on his laptop for what felt like hours, even though it had only been thirty minutes. According to the research he was undertaking, statistically speaking very few houses in the UK had cellars. If the information on the screen was accurate, only a small percentage of properties in England had basement rooms, especially those built after the 1960s.

There were a number of reasons for this. The main one was due to the water table in certain areas. It was almost impossible to dig out a room underneath a house if the hole kept filling up with water. The annual rainfall also played a part in the number of cellars in a particular area.

The information Smith was looking at wasn't helping him, but he wasn't sure how to proceed. Where did they go from here? Somewhere in a cellar in the city three men were being held captive by a woman who wouldn't think twice about letting them die in there. Somewhere in Murton there was a basement room with three homeless men in it. Three men who would probably die if they weren't found in time.

DI Smyth interrupted Smith's research and for once Smith was glad of the distraction.

"The DCI has given the green light for a more extensive search of Murton," DI Smyth said.

Smith rubbed his eyes and turned to face him. "What about your budget?"

"Screw the budget. The big boss wants results, and those results don't come cheap. Are you up to heading over to Murton now?"

Smith looked at the clock on the bottom right-hand side of the laptop. It was just after six.

"It's pitch black out there, boss."

"Are you suddenly afraid of the dark?" DI Smyth said.

"I'm more shit scared of the light to be honest," Smith admitted. "I'm saying a full-on search would be better during the day. Everything looks different under cover of darkness."

"I suppose you're right. It's been a long day, and I could do with a decent nights' sleep. The Super wants a press conference."

"When doesn't he? We don't have anything to give the public yet."

"That's what I told the DCI."

"Although it might not be a bad idea to keep them in the loop," Smith said. "Perhaps we ought to warn the homeless people."

"How?" DI Smyth said. "The last time I looked, the men and women on the streets didn't carry television sets around with them."

"No, but most of them will have mobile phones. I agree that a press conference is a dumb idea right now, but we can still put out some kind of warning on social media."

"Do you think this is the end of it?"

"No," Smith replied without thinking. "Seven men have been imprisoned in cellars in the space of a few weeks. Four of them are dead, and I think this is just the start of something big. A warning to the homeless could make it harder for this *Mother* woman to coerce someone else. Total transparency and all that bull."

"You could have a point. I'm heading home for the day. I suggest you do the same."

"I've got a hot date with a shrink at eight," Smith told him.

"I thought you'd been cleared for duty."

"She wants to pick my brains for some research she's doing."

"Poor woman. She doesn't know what she's letting herself in for."

"She certainly doesn't," Smith agreed. "I presume you haven't had any more nasty surprises from wannabe blackmailers."

"Not a sausage. Whatever you did seemed to have done the trick."

"Glad to hear it," Smith said. "Have you given any more thought about getting it out in the open?"

"Now isn't the right time."

"No worries. I'll see you back here bright and early in the morning."

"I think it'll be better to head straight to Murton tomorrow, first thing," DI Smyth said. "Enjoy your date with the shrink."

Smith shut down his laptop and stretched his arms. The headache was abating – the painkillers had done the trick. He turned off the light and left the office. He debated whether to phone Dr Vennell and reschedule the appointment but decided not to. There was something bothering him, and she might be able to help him with it.

Whitton was talking to Baldwin by the front desk when Smith got there. The two women had always been close. Things had taken a turn for the worse a few years back when Smith had made a terrible decision one night, but the air had cleared since then and Whitton and Baldwin were good friends again.

"Are you ready to head home?" Smith asked Whitton.

"In a bit," she said. "My parents have asked if we want to come for tea."

"I can't. I have a date."

"Since when?"

"Since she phoned me earlier."

"Poor woman," Whitton said.

"Aren't you even going to ask who I'm seeing?"

"No."

"It's Dr Vennell," Smith told her anyway.

"The psychologist?"

"At the last session she asked if I could help her with some research she's doing. Something about serial killers."

"Sounds like it'll be a fun evening," Whitton said.

"You're welcome to join us."

"I'll pass, thank you."

"Are the girls going with you to your parents' place?"

"Laura is sleeping over at Victoria's," Whitton reminded him. "And Lucy has invited Darren round."

"But they'll be in the house by themselves."

Whitton snorted. "I'd say the damage has already been done, wouldn't you?"

Smith couldn't argue with that. "Fair point. Are you heading straight to your parents'?"

Whitton nodded.

"I'll go home and feed the dogs then," Smith said. "And maybe see if a shower can help wash this day off me."

CHAPTER THIRTY

Dr Vennell wasn't there when Smith arrived at the Hog's Head and Smith wondered if she'd forgotten about meeting him. He didn't think she would – she'd seemed very keen to talk to him. She was probably running late. He walked up to the bar and ordered a beer from a man he didn't recognise. The barman poured the pint of Theakston and set it down on the counter.

"Are you new here?" Smith asked.

"First night," the man said. "That'll be four-fifty."

"Four-fifty?" Smith repeated.

"Is there a problem with that?"

"Last time I was here it was four pounds."

"Well now it's four-fifty. Inflation and all that."

Smith nodded and handed him his credit card.

The barman sighed very loudly. "Don't you have cash?"

"I always pay by card," Smith told him. "Marge usually runs up a tab."

"Well Marge isn't here."

"Where is she?" Smith asked.

"She's not feeling too great."

Smith looked at the credit card. "Are you going to make me pay now, or can I run a tab? I'm waiting for a friend, and we'll probably be ordering food."

"I suppose so," the barman said and turned his attention to another customer at the bar.

Smith took his drink to a table and sat down. His phone started to ring and when he glanced at the screen and saw it was Dr Vennell he assumed his initial suspicions were correct – she was calling to tell him she was running late.

He was wrong. She was phoning him to ask where the Hog's Head was. She'd keyed the name of the pub into her Satnav and the GPS had taken her to the other side of the city. Smith gave her the directions and was told she would be there in ten minutes.

A waitress Smith knew well approached the table.

"Will you be having anything to eat?" she asked.

"Probably later," Smith told her. "I'm waiting for someone. Who's the new bloke behind the bar?"

"Pete. He's the new bar manager."

"What about Marge?" Smith wondered. "I thought she managed the bar."

"She brought him in from the agency to take some of the pressure off her. He's supposed to have come highly recommended. For what it's worth."

"I get the impression you don't like him much."

"He's only just started, so it's hard to tell yet. I'll bring you a couple of menus. Can I get you another pint?"

Smith drained what was left in the one he had and gave her the glass. "Thanks."

Dr Vennell walked in fifteen minutes later. She was dressed casually in a pair of jeans and when she took off her coat Smith saw she was wearing a Jimi Hendrix T-Shirt. He was impressed. She spotted him and walked over to his table.

"Sorry I'm late. The GPS in the car took me to some biker pub."

"I've never trusted those things," Smith said. "Well, you're here now. Can I get you something to drink?"

"I'm driving," Dr Vennell said. "But I suppose one pint won't hurt."

"I like the T-Shirt," Smith said when the drinks had arrived. "I didn't have you pegged for a Hendrix fan."

"I'm not really. It used to be my brother's. He died in Berlin a couple of years ago."

"I'm sorry to hear about that."

"It's a long story," Dr Vennell said. "And we're not here to talk about me, are we?"

"Are you hungry?" Smith asked.

"Starving. What would you recommend?"

There was only one thing Smith *could* recommend. As long as he'd been coming to the Hog's Head, there was only one item on the menu that he'd eaten. He told Dr Vennell as much and they were informed that the steak and ale pies would take thirty minutes.

"So," Dr Vennell said. "How was your day?"

"Good," Smith said. "And bad. It's good to be back at work but it's always the same in the early stages of a murder investigation. We get a shitload of information to sift through but only a fraction of that info is relevant to the case."

"Is this about the cellar thing?"

"News spreads fast."

"This is 2020. News is instant these days. What do you know so far?"

"I'm not sure I can tell you too much," Smith said. "There's no patient/doctor confidentiality anymore – you're not officially my psychologist, are you?"

"I don't make a habit of betraying a confidence."

"I thought you wanted to talk about the Ghosts case."

"Hint taken."

"I don't do hints," Smith told her. "But there isn't much to tell anyway. The four Albanian men aren't the only victims in this. We have reason to believe there are three homeless men imprisoned somewhere in the city, and unless we find them, they're going to suffer the same fate as the Albanians. We have very little to go on in the way of leads and I'm still in the dark where the motive is concerned."

"That's very important to you, isn't it?"

"It ought to be important to every detective in the employ of the police,"

Smith said. "Motive is the key element in every murder investigation. What makes these people kill? You mentioned something similar yourself."

"Give me some more," Dr Vennell said.

Smith didn't think he should but there was something in the mannerisms of this young woman that made her very easy to talk to. Smith wondered if her training was the reason for this. He felt like he could trust her."

He ordered another round of drinks and returned to the table.

"Where were we?"

"I want to know more about this cellar thing," Dr Vennell said. "What do you think is happening here?"

"I think it's some kind of experiment," Smith told her. "The victims are chosen simply because they're not going to be missed. Illegal immigrants and homeless men are ideal targets. They're promised board and lodgings and they're also paid well for participating in the experiment. For someone in their position it's an offer too good to refuse. That's how they're persuaded to go down to the cellar. Most people would run a mile, but for these people it's like being given a free room in a hotel for a week. But they have no idea what's in store for them afterwards. The electricity and water is switched off and they're left in darkness to die from dehydration."

Smith took a long drink of beer.

"Those are the bits we do know," he continued. "What we don't know is why are they being subjected to this kind of treatment? What could somebody hope to gain by doing this?"

"An experiment," Dr Vennell mused.

"That's what it's looking like," Smith said.

"It sounds like something out of the dark ages of psychiatry."

"Are you saying something like this has happened before?"

"In the nineteenth century and the early years of the twentieth century there were certain practices that seem absolutely barbaric these days. Even as recently as ten years ago there were mental health professionals who believed in sleep deprivation therapy and similar drastic measures. Of course, things have improved but some of the treatments back then were beyond inhumane."

"It still doesn't explain why someone is doing this to these people," Smith said. "Why lock these men up and deprive them of water and light? What's the point?"

Dr Vennell didn't get the chance to dwell on this. The waitress appeared with two steak and ale pies.

"Let's talk about something else while we eat," Smith suggested.

CHAPTER THIRTY ONE

Smith was unaware that while he was tucking into the best steak and ale pie he'd ever tasted a gormless face was looking out from thousands of TV screens, laptops and tablets across the city. Superintendent Jeremy Smyth lived for moments like these. The public-school moron who believed he held authority over the majority of the police officers in York Police had thrown his toys until he finally got what he wanted.

Superintendent Smyth was of the opinion that the press conference was the be all and end all of every case and he maintained that every investigation needed one, whether it was warranted or not. And this time was no exception. He wasn't a man with political aspirations, but it didn't hurt to pander to the whims and caprices of his appointers every once in a while. Chief Constable Robin Cartwright wanted a satisfactory conclusion to the investigation into the deaths of the Albanian illegal immigrants, and if Superintendent Smyth played his cards right, he could be remembered as being an integral part of that.

PC Neil Walker had been reluctant to grant the Superintendent his wishes. As far as he was concerned York Police didn't have anything to offer the public at this stage, but Superintendent Smyth was adamant, and the press liaison officer had no choice but to agree to it. The public-school idiot had been suitably briefed and now PC Walker was hoping and praying that he would follow that brief without deviation.

Only a select few journalists had been invited to the party. PC Walker decided to inform only the top local newspapers and news bloggers. The audience consisted of just three men and two women, but the public appeal would be broadcast to the far corners of the city.

"The emphasis needs to be on warning the homeless people of York," PC Walker told Superintendent Smyth for the third time. "You need to stress the importance of not accepting any out of the ordinary offers of charity."

"I know what I'm doing," Superintendent Smyth insisted. "Is my tie straight?"

"Sir?"

"My tie. How does it look?"

"It's fine, sir. We're live in ninety seconds."

The press contingency consisted of representatives from the York Herald and the York Post as well as three local news bloggers. All five of them had experience of Superintendent Smyth's ramblings and if PC Walker didn't know any better, he would wonder if some of them were present this evening for entertainment value alone. The Superintendent's reputation was legendary.

A minute and a half later the cameras were rolling, and Superintendent Smyth began.

"Good evening, fellow citizens of York."

PC Walker cringed. He couldn't help it. This wasn't the greatest of starts, and the Superintendent's opening words put him in mind of a recent state of the nation speech by an African dictator whose name he couldn't recall.

"I'll keep this brief," Superintendent Smyth continued. "York Police are asking the general public for help in locating this man."

He looked at PC Walker.

"The photo of Henry Banks will be on the screen, sir," the press liaison officer whispered.

"Henry Banks," Superintendent Smyth said. "Disappeared from the streets yesterday. We believe he was with another man – Steve something or other."

This time PC Walker winced.

"We're asking the public for their help. If anyone knows where these men are we'd like you to come forward. It is possible they were approached by a woman, and they subsequently left with this woman. Someone must know where they went, and somebody must have seen them with this woman. Mr Banks was of no fixed abode, and he eked out an existence on the streets. We know that he plied his trade in the tourist areas of the city around the Minister, and he was last seen there yesterday morning. All information will be treated in the strictest of confidence and – this is yet to be confirmed but I have it on good authority that a reward will be offered for any information that proves to be fruitful."

This time PC Walker tapped Superintendent Smyth on the arm. The reward was news to him, and he knew that things had just become a whole lot more complicated. Now they would have every Tom, Dick and Harry calling in with irrelevant information. The officers manning the switchboard were going to be furious. The press liaison officer decided it was time to nip things in the bud.

"Any questions?"

He ignored the resulting glare from Superintendent Smyth.

The woman from the York Post raised her hand. "Do you believe the disappearance of Mr Banks to be connected to the deaths of the Albanian illegals?"

"At this stage," PC Walker got in first. "It's too early to tell, but we're looking into it. It's possible the person who approached Mr Banks is the same person who locked up the Albanian men, but we have no concrete evidence to confirm it."

"Why is York Police so concerned about a few illegal immigrants and a homeless man?"

This question was posed by the man sitting next to the York Post journalist. He ran the most popular news blog in the city. PC Walker had been expecting this question.

"The social status of these men is irrelevant," he said. "York Police does not discriminate where breaking the law is concerned. If these men have been victims of a crime, we will use all the resources at our disposal to investigate this crime. Any more questions?"

"It's looking to me like you're exploiting these unfortunates to satisfy some kind of agenda," the man from the York Herald put forward. His name was James Lowrie and PC Walker knew him as a pig-headed bigot. "I'm not sure I understand what you're insinuating." It was Superintendent Smyth.

"I'm not insinuating anything. It's plain as day. This stinks of something else altogether. You're making a political statement by chucking resources at so-called victims of crime when we all know that none of these *victims* have ever contributed a penny to the coffers of law enforcement."

"These men are my responsibility," Superintendent Smyth told him. "Four of them are dead, and three more are at risk. I would be derelict in my duties if I did not do everything I could to bring those responsible to book."

James Lowrie opened his mouth to speak but Superintendent Smyth beat him to it.

"I'm not finished. The police in this city take every crime seriously. We do not gauge the severity of the crime based on the social status of the victim, nor do we allocate resources thus. When someone is a victim of a crime it doesn't matter whether they're black, white, brown or, in your case a rather disturbing shade of red – all victims are equal in the eyes of the law. I suggest you head back to the drawing board and reassess your ideals, because there really isn't a place for people like you in this world anymore."

The room fell silent. Even the bigoted man from the York Herald was speechless. PC Walker was impressed. He hadn't expected the press conference to go like this. The skin on James Lowrie's face had now turned an unhealthy shade of crimson and PC Walker was worried he was about to suffer a heart attack right there and then.

"I think we've covered everything," he said. "If there are no more questions, we'll wrap things up there. The number to call with any information is on the screen and the phone lines will be open straight after the press conference. Thank you all for coming."

CHAPTER THIRTY TWO

Tens of thousands of people had seen the footage of the press conference by now but Melanie Gregg wasn't one of them. Melanie hadn't been living on the streets long, but she'd been there long enough to understand the unwritten rules of the homeless. There weren't many of them, but those in place had to be obeyed if life on the streets was to be the lifestyle you were forced to live.

Melanie had learned the ways of the streets quickly, and a chance encounter with a woman who called herself Ginnie was instrumental in that. Ginnie had taken Melanie under her wing and given her a quick lesson in how to make the best of a homeless existence. Melanie understood that her intentions weren't purely altruistic – there were ulterior motives at place, but beggars couldn't be choosers and in this case, *beggars* was the operative word.

"Here comes another sucker," Ginnie nodded in the direction of a man in a suit walking towards them.

He looked to be in his mid-twenties and his gait suggested he'd made a detour to the pub before returning home after work.

"What makes you say that?" Melanie asked.

"Ever green. You'll see. He's clearly pissed and that suit probably cost more than I paid for my first car. He'll be one of those young graduate banker types. Loads of money, but not enough time in the real world to develop a thick skin. Those old businessmen can be real tight arses. Treat him to your best smile."

Melanie did, and it seemed to do the trick. The man in the suit slowed as he passed and glanced in her direction. Melanie and Ginnie were sitting on the wall on Micklegate. The river was flowing gently below the Ouse Bridge behind them.

"Evening," Melanie said.

"Evening," the suited man reciprocated.

Ginnie gave Melanie a subtle nudge in the ribs.

"I don't suppose you'd be in a position to help out a couple of ladies down on their luck, would you?"

Ginne had explained to Melanie that the old chestnut of *spare some change?* wasn't popular anymore. People's mindsets had changed over the years and a different approach was required for a successful beggar to make any money nowadays.

Melanie smiled again and removed a few strands of hair from her eyes in order for the man to get a better look at her face. He smiled a half-smile back and put his hand in his pocket. He took out a wallet, and started to count what was inside.

Like taking candy from a baby, Melanie thought.

"I've only got forty quid," the man said.

His accent wasn't that of a Yorkshireman. He was from somewhere much further south. He looked at Melanie then he looked at Ginnie.

"Well?"

"Well what?" Ginnie asked.

"I've got forty quid."

"What are you trying to say?"

"Is forty quid enough?" he asked her. "But I want her."

He extended a bony finger and pointed at Melanie.

She understood what was happening immediately and she didn't like it.

"Well, darling?" he said. "Forty quid is all I've got."

"It's not..." Melanie started.

"I'll settle for a blowjob."

"Fuck off." It was Ginnie. "Fuck off before I make sure you're incapable of receiving a blowjob for the rest of your life."

"Slags," the man in the suit informed them and staggered off in the direction of the city centre.

"What the hell?" Melanie said. "He thought we were…"

"He was a dickhead," Ginnie said. "It won't be the last time that happens."

"God, I didn't think it would be this bad."

"What did you expect, sweetheart? A fairytale?"

"I never expected what just happened."

"Welcome to the streets," Ginnie said. "Forget about him. He's probably on his way to a lonely bachelor pad with only the prospect of a kebab and a games console to look forward to. He might be loaded but he's more of a loser than you and me will ever be."

"I couldn't help overhearing that."

Melanie and Ginnie both stared at the woman who was now standing opposite them. She was a short, squat woman who looked to be in her fifties. A man appeared next to her. He too was similar in age, and there was something strange about him. The beard under the face mask was grey but the skin on his face was the skin of someone much younger. He was dressed in an old-fashioned way with a tweed waistcoat over a woollen shirt. The trousers he was wearing also looked to be made of wool.

"You shouldn't have to deal with men like that," the woman added.

"You get used to them," Ginnie said.

"Do you live on the streets?" It was the man.

He had a rather gruff voice, and Ginnie wondered if this was because of the blue face mask he was wearing.

"Well spotted, mate," she said.

"Do you like it here?"

"Do I like living on the streets? What do you think. Some of us don't get a choice in the matter."

The woman reached inside her handbag and took out a large purse. She removed a wad of banknotes and offered them to Melanie.

"What's this?" Melanie asked.

"Two-hundred pounds," the woman replied. "Fresh from the ATM on Coppergate ten minutes ago."

"What's the catch?" Ginnie said.

"There isn't always a catch, dear."

That was enough for Ginnie. She snatched the money before the strange woman could change her mind.

"It looks like rain," the man observed.

The clouds forming overhead told them he was probably right and there was a definite tang of it in the air.

"What are your plans for tonight?" the woman addressed this question to Ginnie.

Ginnie looked at the cash in her hand. "A night on the town I reckon."

"Would you be interested in a business proposal?"

"What kind of business proposal?"

"A rather lucrative one. I need someone to look after my house for a week. You'll be fed and you'll have a roof over your heads for the duration. Plus there's five-hundred pounds in it. Each."

"Are you having a laugh?" Ginnie said.

The woman frowned at this. "Why would I joke about something like that? No matter – I'll see if I can find someone else to do it. Good evening, ladies."

She didn't even make it two steps before Ginnie's voice stopped her. "Are you for real?"

The woman turned to face her. "I'm asking if you'll look after my house while I take a trip abroad. You look like someone who can be trusted, and my intuition rarely fails me."

"We'll do it," Ginnie said. "Five hundred quid each, you say?"

"That's correct."

"We don't even know your name," Melanie said.

"That's not important," the woman said. "But if you like, you can call me *Mother*."

CHAPTER THIRTY THREE

"That was a good pie."

Dr Vennell put down her knife and fork.

"You've hardly touched it," Smith said.

The steak and ale pie was only half-finished.

"It's beaten me. That was enough to feed two people."

"The portions are pretty large here," Smith admitted.

"I need to use the Ladies," Dr Vennell said. "If you'll excuse me."

"Can I get you another drink?"

"I imagine one more pint won't hurt," Dr Vennell said. "That pie must have soaked up most of the alcohol from the first one."

The table was cleared, and Smith ordered another round of drinks. His phone beeped to tell him there was a message waiting for him. He opened it and saw it was from Whitton. She would be leaving her parents' house soon and she asked him if he needed a lift back from the Hog's Head. Smith typed a short reply telling her he did. He'd walked to the pub, and he didn't feel like walking back as well. It would save him the hassle of phoning for a taxi. Whitton messaged back to inform him she would be there in thirty minutes.

Dr Vennell returned to the table.

She sat back down. "Talk to me about the police murder case."

"Most of it was in the papers," Smith said. "A group of amateur magicians devised a plan to kill police officers to confirm a theory of theirs."

"That sounds rather drastic."

"They were out to prove a point," Smith added. "They claimed it was some kind of social experiment and the aim was to prove that the police would take the murders of their own more seriously than those of non-police."

"And were they correct in this belief?"

"What do you think?" Smith said. "Of course they were. The experiment was pointless, and it ended in the deaths of some good officers. But the fact of the matter is this: whatever we say, we will always work that little bit harder when someone on the job is the victim."

"It's natural to adopt that attitude," Dr Vennell said. "Not only that, it would probably happen without any of the people involved being aware of it. Human nature is designed like that. We are programmed to protect our own species. And that brings me to my next point. The people who carried out these killings – the ones who committed the police murders, what made them do it?"

"I told you," Smith said. "It was part of a sick social experiment."

"Put that to the side. I'm interested in what makes people kill."

"The motive proved to be elusive," Smith remembered. "Because the truth was so abhorrent we didn't even consider it. There's your answer right there. Sometimes people are just plain evil and it's pointless ripping apart the motivation to look for a justification that simply isn't there."

"Are you suggesting that some people are just born evil?"

"I know for a fact there are people who are."

His phone beeped again. Whitton was just about to leave her parents' house.

"It's my wife," Smith told Dr Vennell. "She's coming to pick me up. You have about fifteen minutes left to pick my brains, Dr Vennell."

"I think you can call me Fiona now," she said.

"Fiona it is then. What made you want to become a psychologist?"

"What made you want to join the police?"

"I asked you first," Smith said.

"It's all I've ever wanted to do. Ever since I was a child, I've been fascinated by why people do what they do. What makes a teenage boy living in the same street as another teenage boy different from his neighbour? What drives one of them to end up graduating from medical school while the other boy ends up involved in a life of crime?"

"Plenty of factors," Smith reasoned. "Financial restrictions, parental guidance or lack of it in the case of the second boy. Peer pressure – I could go on all night."

"And I could listen to you all night. But time is running out. Your turn – what made you decide to become a police detective?"

"The short version is I became world-weary at an age when world-weariness isn't exactly healthy. I watched the justice system fail someone I loved very much and I couldn't stand by and not do something to change that."

"What happened?"

"My Gran was mugged," Smith told her. "Outside the Minster. I caught the scumbag responsible, but the damage had already been done. My Gran fell in the attack and broke her hip. She died three weeks later."

"I'm sorry to hear about that. And that's what made you decide to join the police? To stop it from happening to someone else. That's a very noble move, but it's also rather delusional."

"I'm not an idiot," Smith said. "The system is the system, and one man cannot possibly hope to fix it, but the truth is I had to do something. Anything. The man who killed my grandmother had a good lawyer. He got a couple of years and that didn't sit well with me. I was studying law at the time. I'd just completed three years and I was at the top of my class, but I couldn't do it anymore. I quit the law degree and joined the opposition."

Dr Vennell laughed. Smith was really starting to enjoy that laugh.

"You're a peculiar man, Jason Smith. And a rather complicated one. Can I ask one more question about the police murders before your wife comes and takes you away?"

"Shoot," Smith said.

"Why do you refer to it as the *Ghosts* investigation?"

"Because that's what it felt like we were dealing with," Smith explained. "The killers were like ghosts – disappearing and reappearing without us noticing, but then we found out they were trained magicians and it was all sleight of hand. Misdirection. They weren't ghosts. They were sick individuals who killed my colleagues in the name of some twisted social experiment."

"And now you have another similar experiment on your hands."

"This one is different," Smith argued. "I can't see how this one can be justified in any way."

"Then don't even try and justify it."

"How can I not look for justification?"

"Look beyond the realms of what your rational mind is programmed to do. I'm sure you've done it before."

"I suppose I have," Smith said. "You're telling me not to waste time dwelling on rational reasons and hunt for some irrational ones."

Dr Vennell didn't get the opportunity to comment on this. Whitton had arrived at the Hog's Head - she was standing next to their table and the expression on her face was one Smith didn't like at all.

CHAPTER THIRTY FOUR

The first part of the drive home passed in silence. Smith wasn't quite sure what he'd done wrong, but the cold treatment he'd received at the Hog's Head told him he must have done something. He wasn't in the mood for an argument, so he didn't press the matter. Whitton broke the silence when they were halfway back.

"You didn't tell me your shrink was a teenager."

"She's not a teenager," Smith said. "She's twenty-nine. She looks young for her age."

"And you certainly neglected to inform me she was so pretty."

"I hadn't noticed."

"Is she even qualified?" Whitton wondered. "She doesn't look much older than Lucy."

"She's twenty-nine," Smith repeated. "And she is very qualified. What's wrong with you?"

"What's wrong with me? You're the one out gallivanting with someone who looks young enough to be your daughter."

"Is something wrong?" Smith asked.

"Besides just walking into the Hog's Head and finding my husband sharing a table with a beautiful young woman?"

"I told you I was meeting her," Smith said. "You were invited to join us. Come on, Erica, what's going on?"

"Nothing."

Smith was hopeless at reading women, but he did know it was better to keep his mouth shut when the *N* word was spoken.

The dogs weren't their usual boisterous selves when Smith and Whitton went inside the house. Theakston and Fred wagged their tails in greeting then made a beeline for the living room. Smith wondered if they could sense the tension in the air. He offered to make some coffee and Whitton nodded. She went upstairs to use the bathroom and came back down a few minutes later.

Smith handed her a cup of coffee. "What's this really all about?"

Whitton sat down at the table. "I'm sorry."

"What's wrong, Erica? Is it something to do with your mum and dad? Are Harold and Jane alright?"

"I'm worried about them," Whitton said.

She took a sip of her coffee.

"Talk to me."

"They've been watching the updates on the Covid-19 virus non-stop," Whitton said. "And it's getting serious. The rumours about schools closing and lockdowns are not just rumours. It's going to happen."

"We still don't know that yet."

"It's happening, Jason. China has basically shut down. People are being forced to stay at home. They're not even allowed out on the streets and the same measures are going to be implemented here. I won't be able to see my mum and dad. Laura won't be able to visit her grandparents or her friends."

Smith hadn't really thought about it. The cellar investigation had preoccupied his time.

"I still can't imagine that the government will enforce such drastic measures," he said. "How are people supposed to earn a living if they're not allowed to leave the house?"

"Economists are predicting a financial meltdown if the restrictions are made mandatory. The government is downplaying it. They claim the majority or work can be done remotely these days anyway, and those people who can work from home are being encouraged to do so as soon as possible. They reckon this could come into effect in as little as two weeks' time. York as we know it isn't going to be the same again."

"I need a smoke," Smith said. "I'm finding it hard to get my head around this."

"I'll come out with you."

"What is this going to mean for us?" Smith asked outside in the back garden. "What about the emergency services? We can't work from home."

"We're considered essential workers," Whitton said. "We'll be allowed to carry on working, but we'll have to make some changes. Face masks will have to be worn at all time and contact will need to be kept to a minimum."

"I've never heard something so ridiculous in my life," Smith said. "How are we supposed to arrest scumbags if we're not allowed to make contact with them?"

"I'm just telling you what I've heard."

"It's pointless worrying about something that hasn't happened yet," Smith decided. "Can we talk about something else? Did you really think Dr Vennell was pretty?"

"She's gorgeous, Jason. Is there something wrong with you?"

Smith shrugged his shoulders. "Must be. Or maybe I don't notice shit like that anymore. I'll make sure I take a closer look at her next time I see her."

"Are you going to see her again?"

"You know me, my dear," Smith said. "Me and shrinks have never quite seen eye to eye, yet I always seem to attract them. Besides, I think this one might come in useful."

"What exactly did you talk about tonight?"

"We were supposed to be discussing the *Ghosts* case, but the topic of conversation didn't stay there for too long. We hit on the cellar thing, and she got me thinking."

"I hope you didn't tell her too much," Whitton said. "You could get into trouble."

"She's bound by the nutjob/shrink thing."

"Very politically correct. And she isn't bound by any confidentiality pledge. You're not her patient anymore."

"Anyway," Smith said. "Before you made your dramatic entrance, we were talking about looking beyond the realms of what the rational mind is programmed to look at. Consider the irrational."

"An irrational motive?" Whitton said. "We've come across plenty of them."

"Exactly. And I think we've got another one here."

"I'm going to bed," Whitton said and qualified this with an impressive yawn.

"Me too," Smith said. "We've got an early start in Murton tomorrow."

Whitton put her hand on his shoulder. "Sorry again about tonight."

"It's alright," Smith told her. "Everything will be alright."

"Did you really think my entrance into the Hog's Head was dramatic?"

"I wasn't the only one who noticed it," Smith said. "The poor old bastard sitting next to us moved tables when he saw the look on your face."

CHAPTER THIRTY FIVE

The three men trapped in the cellar in Murton didn't know that the sun had just come up to the east of the city. Marcus, Henry and Steve didn't even realise that it had set some ten hours earlier. For them, trapped in their prison of darkness day and night were now obsolete. The rotation of the earth didn't exist for them anymore.

With the loss of light came a heightened awareness of sound and smell. The stench inside the cellar was now putrid and the heat wasn't helping matters. It was sweltering down here and the stink of human sweat was assaulting the nostrils of the three homeless men, as was the rank odour of foul breath and the unflushed excrement in the toilet close by.

Steve Floyd had been sick in the night. He'd been drifting in and out of sleep when the explosion of vomit had come from nowhere. He'd managed to sit upright quickly enough to prevent the bile from choking him to death, but he was left exhausted in the aftermath. He was so weak now he had no strength to even get up from the floor.

Henry Banks was faring slightly better. As his eyes began to adjust to the darkness his brain was formulating plan after plan inside his head. There had to be a way out of this, and Henry refused to simply lay down and let nature take its course. That wasn't an option for a man who'd spent the majority of his adult life living on the streets. There had to be a way out of the cellar.

Marcus Green was considering everything from a scientific perspective. The medical student understood more than most how the human anatomy worked but that knowledge was proving to be more of a curse than a blessing right now. There wasn't a drop of water left inside the cellar and Marcus knew that horrific things were going to happen to all three men.

The dry mouths they were experiencing now would pale into insignificance compared to what was to come. Their throats would literally dry up and the reserves of saliva would follow suit. Nothing they tried would fix this. Food wasn't an option down in the depths of this hell. All that was on offer was dried produce and that would only expedite the dehydration process further.

On the second day without water the organs would announce their displeasure in the form of devastating cramps. The kidneys would groan and swell to triple their size, and this would be accompanied by excruciating pains. The brain would start to play tricks on them, and their delirium would make them behave irrationally.

After three days, if any of them lasted that long death would be near. It would be lingering in the wings, waiting and all three men would welcome it. By then they would be begging for the end to come.

Marcus was brought out of his morbid reverie by a sound nearby. It was loud and he wondered if his mind was already playing tricks on him. Had he gone without water for longer than he initially thought? He reckoned he had, because the noise still ringing inside his ears sounded like a car door being slammed close by.

He heard it again and his hopes were dashed in an instant. Steve Lloyd coughed his hacking cough once more and everything was quiet again.

* * *

"Did you have to slam the door so hard?" Whitton asked Smith.
They were standing next to her car outside a row of houses in Murton.
"Sorry," he said. "Force of habit. I have to give the door on the Sierra a real shove to get it to close."
"Well, my car is twenty years newer and slightly more expensive to fix than yours. Just don't do it again."
Smith didn't say anything further. Instead, he walked up to the other car that was parked on the road. It was DC Moore's prized Subaru. The man from London got out and stretched his arms.

"Late night?" Smith asked him.

"Early morning," DC Moore said. "I didn't sleep much. I couldn't stop thinking about those blokes locked in the cellar with no food and water. That must be the worst way to die. Locked in the dark and just waiting for it."

"Don't think too much about it."

"Did you see the press conference?"

"It wasn't on my list of things to do," Smith said. "What did old Smyth do this time?"

"He was really good, Sarge. He was on top form. He made one of the local journos look like a right dick, and he did it in style."

"I'll dig it up and have a watch when I get time. Where are the others?"

"DS Bridge is having car troubles," DC Moore said. "So much for his reliable Toyota. And Kerry and the DI are on their way."

"Which of the properties are we interested in?"

"There are six houses with cellars in Murton. Five of them happen to be on this street, and they're all on the same side of the road. According to the plans from the Deeds Office these properties were all built in the same year – back in 1956, and cellars were more popular back then."

DC Moore took out a piece of paper and handed it to Smith. "They're all on there."

The rest of the team joined them fifteen minutes later. Bridge was in his Toyota and the trouble with the car appeared to be nothing serious. The battery cable had somehow come loose, and the problem was easily rectified. DI Smyth decided they would split into teams of two and take two houses each. The uniformed officers who had carried out the initial searches hadn't looked extensively, and it also transpired that two of the houses had been unoccupied at the time, and the two PCs hadn't been able to check these.

Smith told DC King they would take a look at one of these houses first. Number 31 Norton Road was a typical 1950s build. The three-storey semi-detached property stood on a fairly large stand, and the garden looked well cared for.

Smith rang the bell, and the door was opened shortly afterwards by a man dressed in a boiler suit. His eyes were puffy and red, and his skin was very pale.

Smith checked the name on the list. "Mr Peebles?"

"That's me," the man said. "Jacob Peebles. Can I help you?"

Smith took out his ID. "DS Smith, and this is DC King. Can we come inside?"

"I was about to hit the sack. I've just come off a night shift and it ran over for two hours. What's this about?"

"It really would be better to talk inside," DC King told him.

"I suppose you'd better come in then."

"We're you at home yesterday?" Smith asked in the living room. "Around lunchtime?"

Jacob nodded. "I was. I got home about six in the morning and went straight to bed."

"Two of our colleagues knocked on your door yesterday," DC King said. "Why didn't you answer?"

"I was asleep. I probably didn't hear them."

"Are you a deep sleeper?" Smith said.

"Always have been. What are you doing here? I haven't done anything wrong."

"You have a cellar in the house, is that right?"

"I hardly ever go down there."

"Would it be OK if we took a look at it?" Smith asked.

"What on earth for?"

"Just to put our minds at rest."

"Do I have a choice?" Jacob said.

"Yes," Smith said. "We can't force you to let us look down there, but if you refuse, we'll come back with a warrant, and that will be a waste of all of our time. We just want to have a quick look."

Jacob got to his feet. "Come on then."

The door to the stairs leading down to the cellar was locked. Jacob turned the key, pushed open the door and flicked the light switch.

"After you, Kerry," Smith said.

"Thanks a lot, Sarge," DC King said and started to descend the stairs.

There wasn't much down there. An old bicycle with two flat tyres was propped up against one of the walls. There were a number of dust covered boxes, an ancient TV set and very little else. There was nothing to suggest that anybody had been living down there. Smith and DC King walked back up the stairs, Smith thanked Jacob Peebles and they went outside.

Smith's phone started to ring. The ringtone told him it was Grant Webber.

"Webber," Smith answered it.

"I've got something for you," the Head of Forensics said. "A print from the house in Nunthorpe Road."

"I'm listening."

"The owner of the house told you it wasn't him that turned off the electricity, didn't he?"

"He did," Smith confirmed. "He said he didn't turn off the water or the power."

"Billie found one of his prints on the breaker switch on the distribution board."

Smith didn't think this was much of a breakthrough. Arthur Miller was the owner of number 12 Nunthorpe Road, so it wasn't suspicious that his fingerprint was on the DB board. He told Webber as much.

"That's what I said to Billie," Webber said. "But the print was fresh. The owner claimed he hadn't set foot in the house since the end of last month, so how does he explain a print less than a week old?"

"I thought you couldn't determine the age of a print," Smith said.

"You can't be very accurate," Webber explained. "But using mass spectrometry you can narrow it down to a week or so. The residue in the print deteriorates with age and the print on the trip switch wasn't old. Mr Miller was inside that house sometime during the past week."

"Why has it taken so long for you to tell me this?" Smith asked.

"Because we only found the print yesterday. We didn't bother with the DB board when we first arrived on scene. In hindsight we ought to have, but we went back yesterday evening and there it was."

"What do you think it means?" Smith asked.

"You tell me. Your Mr Miller hasn't been telling us the truth, has he?"

CHAPTER THIRTY SIX

Smith was in a positive mood. The public appeal had reaped results and they had a number of positive sightings of Henry Banks to look into. They also had a likely suspect for the first time since the start of the investigation. Arthur Miller was languishing in one of the holding cells while he waited for his solicitor to arrive. Smith had gone straight to DI Smyth, armed with what Grant Webber had discovered and the DI had agreed it was grounds enough to arrest the owner of number 12 Nunthorpe Road.

The team had come up empty handed with the search of the cellars on Norton Road in Murton. None of them were used for anything more than storage, and Smith was starting to wonder if the three homeless men were even in Murton. If they were, they weren't imprisoned in any of the cellars there.

Smith was taking a short break in the canteen. He had the place to himself, and the solace helped him to think. He cast his mind back to the conversation with Fiona Vennell in the Hog's Head. The fresh-faced psychologist had got him thinking. Smith had encountered numerous murderers who killed irrationally, and he knew instinctively this one fell into that category. Spending time considering rational motivation for the imprisonment of men in cellars would be unproductive – they had to look beyond that and consider irrational reasons for the experiments. Nothing occurred to him, but Smith was confident something would come in time.

Whitton came in with Baldwin. They joined Smith at his table.
"Some of the calls that came in last night look promising," Baldwin said. "Did you see the press conference?"
"No," Smith replied. "But I heard the Super was on form. In a good way for a change."
"He left a seasoned journalist speechless," Baldwin said. "The old fossil tried

to make out the police were using the deaths of immigrants and the plight of the homeless men as some kind of political tool, and Superintendent Smyth put him in his place. It really was impressive."

"You said we had some promising calls."

Smith wasn't interested in the Superintendent's rare moment of glory.

"We had the usual timewasters," Baldwin said. "The Super mentioned a reward so that didn't help, but a few people remembered seeing Henry Banks on Friday, and one of those thinks he saw him speaking to a woman. We've got his details and he's agreed to meet us later today."

"Do you think he's genuine?" Smith asked.

"He's been homeless for a few months, and he seems to know Henry and his friend Steven Floyd well. I think he's worth talking to."

"What are your thoughts on Arthur Miller?" Smith said.

"He claims he knows nothing about the men in the cellar," Baldwin said. "His print was on the trip switch on the DB board. He told us he hadn't been inside number 12 for weeks, but that print was more recent than that. Billie estimates it got there no longer than seven days ago."

"That doesn't make him a killer though," Whitton pointed out. "He might have simply forgotten about when he was last in the house. And it's not enough to charge him. I'm surprised the DI even gave the go-ahead to have him arrested."

"The print is enough to warrant it," Smith insisted. "It's more than enough to justify bringing him in for further questioning. Arthur Miller is hiding something and when his solicitor arrives, I'm going to find out what that is."

DI Smyth came in right on cue. "Mr Miller's lawyer has arrived."

* * *

After going through the motions for the tape DI Smyth nodded to Smith to indicate he was to lead off. Arthur Miller's solicitor was a young man who didn't look long out of law school. He'd introduced himself as Peter Tyler and he'd informed them that he'd advised his client to answer any questions put to him.

"Mr Miller," Smith said. "Arthur, do you understand why you were arrested?"

"It's outrageous," Arthur said. "I haven't done anything."

"That's what we're here to decide. For the record, you own a property in Scarcroft – number 12 Nunthorpe Road. Is that correct?"

"You know it is."

"For the record," DI Smyth repeated.

"It's one of four houses I rent out in the city," Arthur said.

"When we spoke last," Smith carried on. "You told us you hadn't been inside the house for a couple of weeks. Do you still maintain this is the case?"

"I think so."

"We'd like you to think harder. You told me you hadn't visited number 12 since the end of last month. Is that still the case?"

"Yes."

"Are you absolutely sure about that?"

"I am."

"You also claimed that it wasn't you who turned off the electricity and the water supply to the house."

"Of course it wasn't me. Why would I disconnect the power and the water?"

"To save money perhaps," DI Smyth suggested.

"How would it save money?" Arthur asked. "There was nobody living in the house, so there wouldn't be any water or electricity usage. Apart from the fridge of course, but I like to keep that running. It tends to stink a bit when it's off for more than a few days."

"May I ask where this is leading?" It was Peter Tyler.

"We're coming to that," Smith told him.

"Mr Miller," DI Smyth said. "You own four properties in the city. Have you always been a landlord?"

"How is this relevant?" It was Peter Tyler again.

"Arthur," Smith said. "Can you answer the question please."

"I've been doing it for quite a while. Ten years or so. I bought my first property in 2008 during the big slump. Houses were going for a song, and I snapped one up for a bargain. I saw an opportunity and the other three houses soon followed."

"What did you do before that?" Smith asked.

"How is this relevant?" Peter Tyler asked again.

"Arthur," Smith urged.

"I worked as a travelling salesman. IT stuff mostly. I got sick of all the jokes, and I decided to try my hand at real estate instead."

"Jokes?" Smith said.

"Arthur Miller? Salesman? Everyone thought they were the first to joke about it and it got a bit tiring."

Smith had no idea what he was talking about.

"Can you explain how a recent fingerprint of yours found its way onto the trip switch on the distribution board in number 12 Nunthorpe Road?" he asked instead.

Arthur glanced at his lawyer.

"Just answer the question," Peter said.

"I don't know," Arthur told Smith.

"The print got there sometime within the past week," Smith elaborated. "Forensic science has come on leaps and bounds and it's now possible to determine the timeline involved. It's by no means accurate – we can only determine it within a week or so, but in this instance that was enough. You touched that distribution board sometime in the past week. Forensic evidence doesn't lie."

Arthur Miller remained quiet.

"Mr Miller," DI Smyth said. "Is there something you'd like to share with us?"

"Do I have to answer?" Arthur addressed this question to his lawyer.

"I'd like to request a break," Peter said. "I'd like to discuss something with my client."

"We're wasting time here," Smith said. "Arthur, did you turn off the electricity in number 12 Nunthorpe Road?"

"My client is entitled to a break," Peter said.

"I didn't turn the power off," Arthur said very quietly.

"Could you say that once more please?" Smith said. "I don't think the recording device picked it up."

"I didn't turn the electricity off in Nunthorpe Road," Arthur said. "I turned it back on."

Smith was definitely not expecting this.

"When was this?"

"Yesterday afternoon. There were no police outside, so I let myself in with my key and flipped the switch back up. Your lot had left it as it was, and I just wanted to turn the power back on."

CHAPTER THIRTY SEVEN

"Fuck it."

Smith was furious. After the interview with Arthur Miller, he'd gone straight outside and smoked three cigarettes in quick succession. To hell with his efforts to try and cut down – that could wait for another day.

Arthur Miller had been allowed to leave. Smith debated whether to charge him with wasting police time and tampering with evidence, but he decided it wasn't worth the effort. It would be time consuming and when it came down to it – what exactly had Arthur done that was against the law? Turning the power back on in a house he owned was hardly a major crime.

Grant Webber had confirmed that the print had been found on the bottom of the trip switch and that was consistent with the switch being flipped upwards. It had been a wasted morning, and Smith was fuming. They were back to square one. Arthur Miller was not the person responsible for locking four Albanians in a cellar.

"What now, Sarge?" DC King asked.

"We focus on the information we got from the public appeal," Smith told her. "We've had a few reported sightings of Henry Banks and one confirmed sighting of Henry talking to a woman. That's the one I want to look more closely at. His name is Martin Southgate and he's agreed to meet at one."

"Is he not coming into the station?"

"He told Baldwin he'd prefer not to. She got the impression he's not a big fan of police stations. He's agreed to meet us at a coffee shop in Bootham."

"Is this going to cost me more money?" DC King wondered. "I'm still fifty quid down from last time."

"And I told you I'd pay you back. Or you could just put in a claim for expenses. I've got it on good authority that the budget has just been increased."

"Do you have any idea how long an expenses claim takes? And the people who took my cash didn't exactly issue receipts."

"I'll pay you back," Smith promised. "I'm just going to grab a bite to eat before we head out to Bootham. I suggest you do the same."

* * *

"I think one of them is dead."

Mother and her partner were staring at the images on the screen of the laptop. The footage was so grainy it was almost impossible to determine what was happening in the cellar in Murton, but the sound was still clear, and the silence told a story of its own.

"The one called Henry said Steve is not breathing," Mother said. "That was an hour ago. I think he's dead."

"He didn't last long at all."

"It's disappointing. Very disappointing. I imagined they'd do better than this."

"We might have a problem with the young woman," Mother's friend said. "She might go to the police."

"She won't," Mother insisted. "She ran long before we got to the house. She got cold feet a long way from the place her friend is now securely locked inside. Even if she does report us to the police, what exactly is there to report? She won't be a problem."

"Are we going to take someone else? Are we going to give the street woman some company?"

"No." Mother said this without thinking. "It will benefit the overall experiment if we observe how well a solitary soul copes under the conditions down in the cellar. It will put a different perspective on things. Do we survive longer in a pack, and does the herd help or hinder us? It's an interesting concept, don't you think?"

"The teenagers are going to be tricky."

"I've got it under control," Mother said.

"Why does it have to be those particular adolescents? Surely there are easier targets."

"It has to be them. It is imperative that it's them, and I know exactly how we're going to take them."

CHAPTER THIRTY EIGHT

Martin Southgate was already there when Smith and DC King arrived in Bootham. The Café Noir wasn't exactly doing a roaring trade this Sunday afternoon and the homeless man was one of only two patrons in the coffee shop. The other customer was a young woman engrossed in something on a mobile phone.

"Mr Southgate?" Smith enquired.

The man in the scruffy tracksuit looked up at him from his seat. "That's me."

Smith sat down next to him. DC King took a seat too.

"Can I get you something to drink?" Smith asked. "Something to eat maybe?"

"A cappuccino and a muffin would be great."

Martin looked to be in his thirties. The grubby tracksuit aside, the impression Smith got was of a man who liked to take care of himself. His hair looked clean, and his complexion was clear. He didn't smell particularly bad, and his blue eyes were bright.

Smith caught the attention of the waiter and ordered the cappuccino and muffin and two coffees.

"Thank you for talking to us," he told Martin. "We appreciate it. Have you been homeless for long?"

"I'm not homeless," Martin said. "I'm just a bit down on my luck right now. I'll get back on track in no time."

"Where are you staying at the moment?" DC King said.

"I've got a place at the shelter in Heweth. They're good people."

"How long have you been there?" Smith asked.

"A couple of months. That's actually where I met Henry?"

"Henry Banks?"

Smith recalled Henry mentioning something about a shelter when he met him in the car park.

"He left the shelter a few weeks ago," Martin added. "He couldn't handle the lack of privacy."

"But you like it there?" DC King said.

"Like I said, they're good people. They don't judge you. Most people don't choose to be homeless. Everybody has their own story and the people running the shelter appreciate this. What is it you want to know?"

The coffees and muffin arrived. Martin tucked in with gusto and the chocolate muffin was devoured in seconds.

"You called the hotline about Henry Banks," Smith said. "You told the operator you saw Henry with a woman. Is that right?"

"I saw them, yes."

"Can you remember what day that was?"

"It was Thursday I think," Martin said. "No, Friday."

"What time was it?"

"Early afternoon. Probably around three. I thought she was just a good Samaritan type. Henry was in his usual place around the corner from the Minster and I just thought the man and woman were stopping to give him some cash."

"There was a man there too?" DC King said.

"It looked like they were together," Martin said. "But it also looked like the woman did most of the talking."

"Did you go and see what was going on?" Smith said.

"Of course not. I know the rules."

"Rules?"

"Think of it as a business transaction," Martin explained. "You do not interrupt a deal in progress. It's bad form on the streets. I was going to wait until the man and woman were gone before I went and had a chat with

Henry, but he left with them. Him and that oddball friend of his."

"Steve?" Smith guessed.

"That's him."

"Don't you like him?" DC King said.

"He's just odd. There's something not right about the bloke."

"Which direction did they go?"

"Towards the Hull Road."

This made sense. Hull Road was to the east of the Minster and that's the direction you would head in if you wanted to go to Murton.

"Can you remember what the man and woman looked like?" Smith asked.

"I didn't really get a good look at them," Martin said. "She was pretty old, I think. Mid-fifties perhaps, and she was a bit on the porky side. And short with it. Brown hair."

"What about the man?" DC King said.

"Probably the same age as her. Grey beard. You couldn't see half of his face because of the mask, but I could see strands of a grey beard.

"He was wearing a face mask?" DC King said.

"A blue one," Martin said. "Like a surgeon's mask."

"Why would he wear a face mask?" Smith wondered.

"The experts have been advising people to wear them," DC King told him. I've seen a few people wearing them."

"Is there anything else you remember about the man and the woman?" Smith asked Martin.

"That's all I can tell you."

"You've been a great help," Smith said.

The description Martin had given them of the man wasn't even close to what Arthur Miller looked like. It hadn't been a mistake to release the owner of number 12 Nunthorpe Road.

"What happened to him?" Martin said. "Is Henry in some kind of danger? The appeal last night was really creepy."

"We're not sure what's going on yet," Smith said.

"I get it," Martin said. "You're not allowed to tell me anything, but I'm not stupid. You don't make an appeal like that without good reason. You're warning homeless people not to accept any unusual offers from strangers. It doesn't leave much to the imagination, does it? Is Henry dead?"

"We don't think so. But we believe he's in danger. If you think of anything else, give me a call."

He took out one of his cards and placed it on the table.

"Any time," he added. "Day or night."

The waiter came back and asked them if they wanted anything else. Smith asked him for the bill.

"I'll get this," he said.

"Cheers," Martin said. "I hope you find him. Henry, I mean."

He picked up Smith's card and left without saying anything further.

Smith was waiting for the waiter to fetch the credit card machine when three teenagers came inside the coffee shop. He was surprised to see them – it was Lucy, Darren Lewis and Jane Banks. Lucy spotted him and walked straight over.

"What are you doing here?" Smith asked her.

"They do great coffee here," she said. "And it's cheap."

"Afternoon, Mr Smith," Darren said.

Smith ignored him and turned to Jane. "I didn't know you were into coffee."

"I always have a milkshake," she said. "I can't stand coffee."

"Do you come here a lot?" Smith said.

"Most Sundays," Lucy said. "Don't you pay attention to anything I tell you?"

"I'll try and make more of an effort in the future."

The waiter came back with the credit card machine.

"Add another ten pounds onto the bill for whatever the kids want to order," he told the man. "If it comes to more than ten quid, that's their problem." The waiter thanked him and completed the transaction.

"I'll see you later then," Smith said to Lucy. "We have to get back to work."

"See you later, Mr Smith," Darren said.

Smith ignored him again.

Lucy, Darren and Jane chose a table by the window. Lucy watched as Smith and DC King walked out and turned left onto St Olave's. She turned her attention back to her friends and didn't see the two people heading for the coffee shop. She didn't see that the woman was watching Smith as he walked off into the distance. The couple stopped by the coffee shop and then the door was opened, and they came inside. Lucy looked up as they passed and the woman gave her a smile. Lucy found herself smiling back. The man she was with was wearing a blue face mask.

CHAPTER THIRTY NINE

"You have to try this," Lucy handed Jane the cup.

"What is it?" Jane said.

"Mochaccino. It's like chocolate flavoured coffee."

"You don't normally drink that," Darren said.

"That's because it's expensive, but my dad paid for this one."

Jane took a tentative sip. "It's actually not that bad. But I'll stick with my milkshake, thank you."

She took a loud slurp through the straw. The strawberry shake was already half finished.

   "I wonder what will happen to this place when the Covid restrictions come in," Lucy said. "They'll have to close until it's all over."

"Do you think it will ever be over?" Jane asked. "Have you seen the latest statistics? It's infecting more and more people every day, and they can't stop it."

"People are dying all over the place," Darren joined in.

"They'll find a way to cure it," Lucy said.

"Aren't you scared?" Jane said.

"Of course I'm scared. I did some research, and they reckon pregnant women are three times more likely to develop severe complications from the virus. I'm worried about the baby. What am I going to do if I get it?"

"The hospitals won't close," Jane said. "They'll make sure the healthcare workers keep working."

"But what if they can't cope?" Lucy put forward. "What if there are so many infected people the hospitals and clinics are packed to the brim? I might even be forced to have the baby at home."

"I won't allow it," Darren told her.

"Listen to you," Jane said. "*I won't allow it*. You sound like a control freak Yorkshireman. This is 2020, Darren dearest – your flat caps and your male chauvinism are so last century."

Darren didn't comment on this. He took something out of his bag and placed it on the table.

"Wow," Jane commented. "Is that what I think it is."

Darren grinned. "It is. You're looking at the new Galaxy Tab S7plus. Twelve and a half inches of viewing pleasure."

Lucy didn't seem impressed. "How did you even afford that? Those things cost almost a grand. I thought you said you were saving the money from your IT jobs for when the baby arrives."

"I am," Darren said. "This was…"

"It was what?" Lucy interrupted. "An essential purchase for the future of your IT career? A bargain?"

"If you'd let me finish," Darren said. "It was a present from my uncle. He knows how much I'm into IT and he got it in Japan. He was over on business, and it was half the price there. I'm saving every penny I make from the computer work – I promise you."

The three friends remained silent for a while. The only sound was the occasional slurp from Jane's milkshake.

"It's the hormones," Jane was the first to speak.

Lucy glared at her, but it didn't last long. He face broke into a smile and then she erupted with laughter.

"You women are weird," Darren said. "You're schizos, all of you."

Lucy was aware of someone standing behind her. She could sense it. She turned around and looked up at the woman standing there. It was the woman who'd smiled at her when she came inside the Café Noir.

"I apologise for interrupting your discussion," she said. "But I couldn't help overhearing. I'm having some problems with my Internet connection at home. I just can't get it to work, even though the service provider says there's nothing wrong with it. I'd really like to talk to my sister in Canada on that new Skype thing but I can't figure it out."

"Are you using a wireless router?" Darren asked her. "Or is it a satellite signal?"

"I'm afraid you lost me at router, young man."

"What does it look like? Is it a small boxlike thing with antennas?"

"I think so."

"And you're sure it's plugged in right?" Darren said. "Sometimes the sim gets dislodged. What are the dots on the display showing?"

"I really don't know much about it. Would it be possible for you to take a look at it? I'll pay you of course."

"All you need to do is check the router," Darren said. "It's not a major job."

"He'll do it." It was Lucy.

"What?" Darren said.

"You said yourself it's not a complicated job."

"That would be wonderful," the woman said. "I see you've finished your drinks. Allow me to get the bill."

"It's already paid for," Jane said.

"You want me to do the job now?" Darren asked.

"If you could. It's my sister's birthday today and it would be lovely to wish her happy birthday on Skype."

"I didn't realise you meant now," Darren wasn't quite finished yet.

"Please. If you can get the Internet up and running and set up my Skype I'll pay you Sunday rates. How does a hundred pounds sound."

"It sounds very generous," Lucy replied for her boyfriend.

"I'll need the address," Darren said.

"It's not far," the woman said. "My friend can give you a lift. His car is parked right outside."

"I don't know," Darren said. "I shouldn't really get in cars with strangers."

"I'd say we're well enough acquainted, wouldn't you? Besides, your friends can come too. You really will be helping me out a lot."

"OK," Lucy agreed.

"Thank you. As I said you will really be helping me out a lot."

CHAPTER FORTY

Smith was unsure how to proceed. So far the day had been rather unproductive. They hadn't found anything in any of the cellars in Murton to suggest that anybody had been imprisoned there – the conversation with Martin Southgate hadn't given them anything to go on, and they were still no closer to learning the whereabouts of the three homeless men. Time was running out. If Smith's suspicions were correct and the three men had been imprisoned by the same woman who caused the deaths of the Albanians, time was a luxury they didn't have.

And where did the man fit into the equation? The Albanians referred to someone called Mother in the journal but there was no mention of a man. Who was this man? The descriptions Martin had given them were very vague, and Smith didn't know where to look next.

"What's the plan of action, Sarge?" DC King asked.

They were standing next to Smith's car in Bootham.

"I don't have one, Kerry," he admitted. "It's looking to me like Baldwin was mistaken when she thought the man who called said he was in Murton. We've checked all the cellars in that part of the city, and we found nothing. The men must be somewhere else. We need to widen the search."

"Are you suggesting we search every cellar in York? Do you realise how long that will take?"

"Do you have any other suggestions?"

DC King's silence told him she didn't.

"Three men are almost certainly going to die unless we find them," Smith carried on. "Three homeless men will perish in the most horrendous way possible unless we locate them before tomorrow. For all we know it might already be too late, but we have to keep looking."

"I agree with you, Sarge," DC King said. "We can't stop. Not only to save their lives. If we get to the men in time, we might get some answers as to who did this to them."

"I want to know why," Smith said. "The motive is still eluding me, and I get a bit pissed off when that happens."

He took out his cigarettes and lit one.

"You're not smoking as much as you usually do," DC King commented.

"I'm trying to cut down," Smith told her. "The doctors reckon my heart isn't as strong as it was after it stopped for a minute and a half. I don't feel it – it seems stronger than ever, but who are we to go against doctor's orders?"

"We will find them, Sarge," DC King promised. "We'll find these men and we'll also find your motive."

"It's bugging me. We know it's some kind of experiment, but there has to be more to it than that. The concept of the experiment feels a bit off to me. There's something else to it, but I can't for the life of me figure out what that is."

The sound of his phone cut short the conversation. He took it out and saw it was work.

"Smith," he answered it.

"We might have something to look into, Sarge." It was Baldwin.

"Go on."

"There's a woman here who thinks her friend has been abducted. Her name is Melanie Gregg and she came in after watching a repeat of the appeal. Melanie and a woman called Ginnie were approached by a man and a woman yesterday. The woman gave them two-hundred pounds and offered them much more if they would housesit for a week."

"Do you think it's connected to the investigation?"

"I don't know, Sarge," Baldwin said. "But it's worth looking into. Melanie got a bad feeling about things – she made this clear to her friend, but Ginnie wouldn't listen. Melanie ran off but Ginnie went with the man and woman. It could have been a trap."

"It could well have been," Smith agreed. "Where is she now? Where is Melanie now?"

"She's still here. I asked her to wait in the canteen until you got back. I think it's worth speaking to her."

"I do too. We'll be back as soon as we can. Thanks, Baldwin."

"That sounded promising," DC King said.

"It could be," Smith said. "I think this *Mother* woman has taken another victim and Melanie Gregg might be able to tell us where her friend was taken. Perhaps I'll get my motive sooner than I thought."

They got in the car and when Smith turned the key in the ignition nothing happened. He tried again with the same result. After the fifth time he admitted defeat. The high-pitched screeching sound told him something was serious wrong.

"It sounds like the starter motor," DC King said. "The coil has probably gone."

"What I know about cars can be written on the back of a postage stamp, Kerry," Smith admitted. "All I know is you have to put petrol in them to make them go."

"It definitely sounded like the starter. It's easily fixed."

"Can you fix it?"

DC King started to laugh. "You'll need to get it towed to a garage, Sarge. When I said it was easily fixed, I meant by a mechanic. It's a three-hour job. Phone your insurance company. If you've got breakdown cover they'll send someone out to help."

"That might be a problem," Smith said.

"You're insured, aren't you?"

"I was, but I think I forgot to pay the latest instalment. It slipped my mind."

"Are you telling me you've been driving around without insurance?"

"It wouldn't be the first time," Smith said.

He finished the cigarette and lit another. "What do you suggest we do now, Kerry?"

"You'll have to phone for a tow truck," she said. "And arrange for someone to come and pick us up. Phone Whitton."

"That's a very bad idea," Smith said. "She'll never let me hear the end of it. You get hold of a tow company, and I'll give Bridge a call."

CHAPTER FORTY ONE

"Here we are," the woman told the three teenagers.

Lucy was wondering why they hadn't walked. The house the car parked outside was in Clifton. It was a five-minute walk from the coffee shop in Bootham.

"We could have walked," the woman said, as if reading her thoughts. "But we had the car anyway. Out you get."

The house they walked towards was one of a row of identical looking properties in a street of semi-detached houses. Number 24 Baker Street was three rows back from the York Hospital and as they got closer it became clear that a keen gardener lived here. The small front lawn was green and healthy looking. It was still mid-March and the grass on the lawns of the neighbouring houses was still brown but the artificial grass in front of number 24 was well tended. The shrubs in the beds were yet to grow but they'd been cut back, ready for the spring.

"Home sweet home," the woman said. "Come in, and make sure to wipe your feet."

"She's weird," Darren whispered.

"She's paying you a hundred quid to flick a switch," Jane reminded him. "Humour her."

"It'll be a five-minute job," Lucy added. "Just smile and wave."

"What are you three conspiring?"

The peculiar woman had turned around and she was looking at the three friends.

"We're just talking about school stuff," Jane lied.

"Glad to hear it. Come in – you're letting the cold air in.

She stood to the side and waited for them to get inside the house. Then she closed the door behind them. The man was nowhere to be seen.

"Where's your router?" Darren asked.

"I keep it plugged in next to my laptop," the woman told him. "I thought it would give off a better signal if I did that."

"Let's see what we've got, shall we."

"Follow me."

The woman led them down the corridor in the direction of the kitchen. She stopped halfway next to a door on the left. She opened it and turned on the light.

"What's down there?" Lucy asked.

"My office and work room. It's where I do all my scrapbooking."

"What happened to the bloke?" Jane said.

"He had things to do."

"And what's the story with the mask?" Darren added.

"He's rather germ phobic, and the impending Covid pandemic is no laughing matter."

"They reckon we'll all have to wear them soon," Jane said.

"That's very true," the woman said. "Everything we thought was normal will cease to be so before we know it. Follow me."

She led them down a narrow staircase into a large cellar. There were no windows but the lights on the ceiling and walls were lighting up the room as if there were. An air conditioning unit was pumping out warm air. There was a leather sofa against one of the walls and a widescreen TV on the wall opposite. A section of the room had been partitioned off with a high screen.

"This is so cool," Darren commented. "I wish I had a pad like this in my house. I'd never leave it. Is that the Xbox E3?"

He pointed to the games console on the cabinet below the television.

"My grandson likes to play down here when he comes to visit," the woman said. "It's impossible to get him to stop playing sometimes."

Lucy suddenly felt cold. The aircon was heating the cellar beautifully, but Lucy wasn't feeling it. The chill spread from her feet, up her legs and stopped in her chest. She put a hand to the bump in her belly.

"Are you feeling OK, dear?" the woman asked.

"I'm fine," Lucy lied.

"When are you due?"

"August," Lucy replied in a voice no louder than a whisper.

"You must be very excited."

This was directed at Darren.

"What?" he said. "How did you know I…"

"Perception comes with experience, my boy."

"Can we just get this done?" Lucy asked. "I have to be home soon."

"Would you like something to drink?" the woman asked. "I keep it nice and toasty down here, but it does make you thirsty after a while."

"No thanks," Lucy said.

"I'll make some lemonade then."

The woman was up the stairs in a flash. She turned around and looked at the three teenage friends.

"I'll leave you in peace to figure out the Internet."

"She gives me the creeps," Lucy whispered.

"She's alright," Darren said. "She's just a bit eccentric."

"And she's paying you a hundred quid for nothing," Jane added.

"Let's see what the problem is with the router," Darren said.

It didn't take long to find out what was wrong. Darren located the router. It was on the desk next to an old laptop. The absence of lights on the display told him it wasn't even plugged in.

Darren told Lucy and Jane as much. "She clearly doesn't know much about technology."

He found a plug socket and inserted the adaptor. The lights flickered to life and then a single red dot could be seen.

"There's no signal down here," Darren deduced. "It's hardly surprising."
He took out his phone. "There's no network coverage either."
Lucy and Jane checked their own phones. Neither of them had signal either.

The woman came back down with a tray of lemonade.
"Are you winning?"
"The router wasn't plugged in," Darren said. "But there's no signal down here anyway. You'll probably have to use the laptop upstairs."
The woman placed the tray on the table. "Can you fix it?"
"I told you," Darren said. "The signal is terrible down here. I'll show you."

He flipped up the screen on the laptop and turned it on. It took forever to warm up.
"It's asking me for a password," he said.
"Password," the woman told him. "*Password* is the password. It means I don't have to remember anything. We have so many passwords these days, don't we? All lower case."

Darren keyed it in and found the Internet settings.
"Do you see? There's no Internet. The signal is just too weak."
"I want you to fix it." The woman's tone had changed.
There was something sinister in her voice now.
"Let's try it upstairs."
"I want you to fix it down here."

Darren closed down the *settings* and something on the screen caught his attention. On the Desktop was a file labelled *Cellar 1*. Beneath it was another file – *Cellar 2*. Darren hovered the arrow over the second one.
"Take a look," the woman said. "If you dare."
"What's going on?" Lucy said.

"Drink your lemonade. And open the file."

Darren clicked on the *Cellar 2* file and a grainy image appeared on the screen.

"What the fuck."

On the screen was a video clip of something none of the friends could quite make out. It showed a dark room. A movement in the corner of the screen caught Darren's eye then a man's face came into the shot. The man's eyes were unblinking and he was staring right into the camera.

"What is this?" Darren asked.

He was talking to himself. He turned around, but the woman was gone.

There was a loud click as the door at the top of the stairs was locked.

CHAPTER FORTY TWO

Melanie Gregg was still in the canteen when Smith and DC King arrived back at the station and Smith was relieved. It had taken him over an hour to get back. A tow truck had taken his old Ford Sierra to a garage, and Bridge had come to pick them up. It wasn't yet clear what was wrong with the car but the mechanic had promised to give Smith a call later in the day with the diagnosis. Smith and DC King had headed straight for the canteen.

Melanie Gregg was the only person present and Smith decided to speak to her there rather than in the sterile environment of an interview room. He would listen to her story and go down the formal route if he decided she had anything important to tell them.

"Sorry it took us so long," he said and sat down opposite the young homeless woman. "Car troubles. Can I get you some coffee from the machine? Contrary to what you might read in crime novels, police coffee doesn't always taste like dishwater."

"I've already had two," Melanie told him.

Smith gauged her age to be around twenty. She was a pretty woman with striking blue eyes. Her hair looked like it hadn't been washed for a few days and there were smudges of dirt on her left cheek. DC King took a seat next to her.

"Thank you for coming in," Smith said. "I believe you're concerned about a friend of yours."

"Ginnie wouldn't listen," Melanie said. "I told her there was something dodgy about the man and woman, but she wouldn't listen."

"Could you talk us through what happened from the beginning," Smith said.

"It was yesterday evening. Late. Probably around nine. We were standing on the bridge by Micklegate."

"That's the Ouse Bridge?" Smith asked.

Melanie nodded. "There was this bloke approaching us. He was a bit pissed and Ginnie was suddenly wide awake. The drunk ones always tend to be more generous. Anyway, we caught his attention and I asked him if he could help us out with a few quid."

"Did you know the man?" DC King.

"What do you think? He was one of those rich city types, and we thought we could pump him for a few quid, but he got the wrong end of the stick."

"What do you mean by that?" Smith asked.

"He thought we were on the game. Thought we were prostitutes. Ginnie quickly told him to sod off then this man and woman suddenly appeared."

"I need some coffee," Smith said.

He got up and walked over to the machine in the corner.

"Go on," he said when he returned to the table.

"The woman told us she couldn't help overhearing and she took out a wad of cash and gave it to us."

"She just handed you some money?" DC King said.

"Two hundred quid," Melanie elaborated. "Fresh from the ATM on Coppergate she said."

"Did you take the money?" Smith said.

"Of course we took the money," Melanie snorted. "But then the woman offered us more if we would look after her house for a week. She said she was going on holiday or something and she needed someone to housesit. She said she would make it worth our while."

"And you agreed?" Smith said.

"It was a no-brainer. She was giving us a roof over our heads for a week, and she was going to pay us for it. I would have done it for nothing. I didn't mention that though."

"I don't suppose you did," Smith said. "Then what happened? What made you change your mind?"

"I don't know," Melanie said. "It was a feeling I started to get. It's hard to explain, but it felt like something wasn't quite right about the whole thing. You know like when something is too good to be true."

"It's often because that's exactly what it is," Smith said. "Where did the man and woman take you? Where was the house?"

"I didn't get that far. I legged it before we'd even got there."

"Were you on foot?" DC King said.

"We walked, yes. We'd got as far as the Museum Gardens, and I whispered to Ginnie that I didn't like it. I suggested we do a runner."

"But Ginnie didn't listen?" Smith said.

"She said it was easy money," Melanie said. "Said I was being pathetic. I told her I wasn't coming with her, and I walked off."

"Did the man and woman try to stop you?" DC King asked.

"They might have called out, but they didn't come after me."

PC Black came into the canteen. Smith gave him a shake of the head and the young PC took the hint. He got some coffee from the machine and left again.

"Can you describe the man and woman?" Smith said.

"She was probably mid-fifties," Melanie said. "Short and squat. Brown hair and she had a weird way of talking."

"What do you mean by that?" DC King said.

"It was like she talked in riddles sometimes. She said strange things."

"What about the man?" Smith said.

"He was probably about the same age as her. Also short with a grey beard. He was wearing a face mask."

Smith knew then that they were onto something. This was definitely the same couple Martin Southgate had described.

"Would you be prepared to work with a police artist?" he asked Melanie.

"I don't know," she said. "I can't really remember their faces very well."

"Our artist is very good at helping you to recall the features," DC King told her.

"I don't know," Melanie said once more. "I couldn't really see much of the man's face because of the mask covering his nose and mouth."

"It's worth a shot anyway," Smith said. "Is there anything else you can remember about them? Had you seen them before?"

"I don't think so. Do you think they're going to hurt Ginnie?"

"Not if we find her in time. And you coming here will help us."

"I'll get hold of an artist," DC King offered. She turned to Smith. "It's Sunday – do you think the budget will stretch to it?"

"Don't worry about that," Smith said.

DC King got up and left the canteen.

"Ginnie is in trouble, isn't she?" Melanie asked Smith.

"She is," he admitted. "We believe these people are extremely dangerous, and it's imperative that we find out where they took Ginnie. You came here because you watched the appeal, didn't you?"

"I saw it in a pub in Skeldergate. That weird policeman spoke about not accepting any charity from a man and a woman. Anything odd, and I immediately thought about the money the woman gave us."

"You did the right thing," Smith said. "We appreciate it. Where are you staying at the moment?"

"Wherever I can. I sometimes crash on the sofa in one of Ginnie's friend's house. I'll probably stay there tonight."

"What about the shelters?" Smith asked.

"They're usually full. I'll find somewhere."

"If you don't," Smith said. "Give me a call. I don't want you sleeping on the streets."

He took out one of his cards and handed it to her.

She picked it up and put it in her pocket. "What are you? Some kind of good Samaritan?"

"I'm just a bloke trying to do the right thing," Smith said. "If you need any help, call me."

CHAPTER FORTY THREE

"I can't take this anymore."

Henry Banks was doubled over in agony. Every muscle in his body was throbbing in time with his heartbeat. He was burning up with fever but he wasn't able to perspire. The remaining moisture inside his body had long drained up, and the sweat glands were straining to produce anything more than foul-smelling pus. Henry's kidneys were shutting down. He hadn't urinated for twenty-four hours, and the toxins were building to dangerous levels. His liver was also on the verge of giving up the ghost.

"I want to die," he said.

"Take deep breaths," Marcus Green advised him. "Breathe in for a few seconds, hold it and breathe out slowly."

"I just want to die," Henry said. "We're both going to die."

Steve Floyd had been dead for a while now and he was starting to smell. Marcus and Henry had left him where he died. He was curled up in a ball on the floor, and his eyes were wide open. Marcus knew instinctively that he and Henry were soon to join him in his permanent sleep. Death was close for both men.

The heat inside the cellar was stifling. Marcus was certain the central heating had been turned up even higher. There was only one radiator down in the depths of the basement room but it was pumping out an awful lot of heat. Marcus looked at Henry. He was shivering now even though his core temperature had reached dangerous levels. His body was losing the ability to regulate its own temperature.

Marcus's gaze turned to the radiator against the wall and an idea started to form in his head. He was taken back to when he was a child. His father had refused to fix a leak in the radiator in the bathroom and he'd paid the price for it. The dripping pipe had burst and flooded not only the bathroom, but the entire carpet on the upstairs landing. Marcus could still recall the hissing sound it made just before the pressure became too much and the pipe burst.

"The radiator is full of water."

He spoke the words to nobody in particular.

"The radiator is full of water."

This time he was addressing Henry. It was a one-way conversation - the homeless man wasn't listening.

He forced himself to walk up to the radiator. It looked brand new and there was no cut off valve. It couldn't be turned off manually. Marcus assumed the temperature was controlled from somewhere else in the house. The pipe coming into the side of the radiator was extremely hot, but Marcus expected it to be. He went to the kitchen area and found a couple of towels. He opened the drawers and picked up a large frying pan. It was a heavy duty pan with a wooden handle, and it might just work for what Marcus had in mind. There was a plastic bowl in the sink and Henry picked this up too.

"This has to work," he told the radiator.

After wrapping one of the towels around the part of the inlet pipe that fed into the radiator Marcus placed the washing up bowl on the floor in front of it. He took aim with the frying pan and smacked the pipe hard. There was a loud crack, but the pipe didn't budge. Marcus tried again and this time it gave a little. Another whack caused a jet of steam to hiss from the pipe. Marcus concentrated hard. He was on the verge of collapsing but he was almost there. He raised the frying pan up in the air and brought it down on the pipe with everything he had left inside him. The pipe burst and a scalding jet of water blasted out.

Marcus directed the flow into the washing up bowl. It filled up in seconds. With a burst of energy that came from nowhere, Marcus rushed to the bath, inserted the plug and emptied the water into it. He raced back to the radiator and repeated the procedure. After a dozen trips back and forth Henry was exhausted. The bath tub was half full and he decided to stop. The water was still too hot to drink but the surface area of the liquid in the bath meant it would cool quickly and Henry estimated it would be palatable in an hour or so. The water was still pouring out of the broken pipe next to the radiator. Marcus ignored the pain as the scalding liquid burned his feet.

Forty-five minutes later and the water hadn't stopped flowing. The whole floor of the cellar was now flooded. Marcus didn't care. He headed to the bath and dipped a finger in. The water had cooled much quicker than he expected it to. He scooped up a glassful and walked over to Henry.
"Drink slowly," he said and held the glass to his lips.
Henry didn't drink. His lips were cracked and dry and they weren't moving.
Henry Banks was dead.

* * *

"We've got a description of the man and woman who abducted a woman by the Ouse Bridge yesterday," Smith began.
The team had gathered for a briefing in the small conference room.
"Melanie Gregg and a woman called Ginnie were approached by the couple yesterday afternoon," he continued. "They were given two-hundred pounds and promised more if they would look after the woman's house for a week. Melanie smelled a rat on the way to the house and ran off, but Ginnie didn't."

"Do we know where she was taken?" DI Smyth asked.
"Unfortunately, not. Melanie left them by the Museum Gardens so we can't be sure where they were going. She's working with an artist as we speak, and hopefully we'll get a good impression of what these people look like. It was definitely the same people Martin Southgate saw talking to Henry Banks. The descriptions matched perfectly. We're looking for a woman in her mid-fifties with brown hair. She's short and plump and she's clearly not short

of cash. The man is also mid-fifties, and he has a grey beard. He wears a surgical mask, and that might help us. There aren't many people walking around with face masks over their nose and mouth."

"What else did Melanie tell you?" Bridge said.

"That's about it. She's never seen them before, and she said they appeared from nowhere."

"They were being watched," DC King suggested.

"I'm inclined to agree. I think they've been scouting for potential victims and they've been keeping an eye on Melanie and Ginnie for a while."

"A citywide search of every cellar in York is out of the question," DI Smyth said. "I put forward your suggestion to the powers that be, and it's just not feasible."

"We need to find those men," Smith said. "They are going to die if we don't find them."

"We're in needle in a haystack territory here, Smith. There just aren't enough hours in the day and officers at our disposal to carry out such a mammoth task. It can't be done."

Smith opened his mouth to say something, but the DI got in first.

"And it is not up for debate," DI Smyth said.

"I'm running out of ideas, boss," Smith said. "We have no idea where those men are and we haven't a clue who took them. All we've got is a couple of witness descriptions of the man and the woman, nothing else."

"We might get lucky with the artist's impression."

"I'm not happy to wait for lady luck to pay us a visit," Smith said. "We need to do something, but I can't think of a way forward. These people are luring homeless people into their dens and waiting for them to die. They're going to carry on doing this unless we stop them."

"We don't know that, Sarge," DC Moore said. "Perhaps they've finished."

"They're not finished, Harry," Smith said. "They're getting a kick out of it.

They're preying on vulnerable people – people who won't be missed, and they're only going to stop when we make them stop. Does anyone have any ideas on how we can proceed?"

"The ATM," DC King said after a few seconds had passed.

"What ATM?" Smith asked.

"Melanie Gregg told us the woman gave her and Ginnie two hundred pounds," DC King elaborated. "Fresh from the ATM on Coppergate."

"CCTV cameras," Bridge had cottoned on.

"Kerry," Smith said. "If my wife wasn't sitting next to you, I would kiss you right now. All the ATMs in the city are monitored by CCTV."

"Melanie said they were approached by the man and woman around nine last night," DC King said. "So we check the footage around that time."

"It might give us a more detailed description of them," Bridge said.

"It'll give us more than that, Sarge," DC Moore joined in. "Once we know from the CCTV cameras exactly what time the cash was withdrawn, we'll be able to get the name of the person whose account the money was withdrawn from."

CHAPTER FORTY FOUR

"I'm scared."

Lucy was looking at the screen on her phone again. There was no mobile phone coverage down in the cellar. The house had gone silent not long after the woman had locked them down there and the three friends didn't know what was happening.

"Where did she go?" Jane wondered.

"I haven't heard anything upstairs," Darren said. "The bitch has locked us down here."

"Do you think it's the same woman who killed those Albanian immigrants?" Jane said.

"I don't think so," Darren said. "She's going after homeless people and people who won't be missed. What time are your parents expecting you home?"

He put a hand on Lucy's shoulder.

"If I'm not back before five they'll wonder where I am," she said. "But if they're busy at work they might be late home."

"What about your sister?" Jane said. "Where is she? She can't be at home by herself."

"Laura is staying over at a friend's house," Lucy said. "She'll go straight to school from Victoria's house tomorrow. I might not be missed for ages."

"Is there no phone signal anywhere down here?" Jane said.

"I've tried," Darren told her. "I've walked the whole room flat and there's nothing."

"Why has she locked us down here?" Lucy said. "We haven't done anything to her."

"She's fucked in the head," Darren said. "We should never have agreed to go with her."

"It's a bit late for that," Jane stated the obvious. "I'm hungry. I wonder if there's any food down here."

There wasn't. The cellar consisted of just one room. There was no kitchen, no bathroom and no sign of any food or water. The lemonade on the tray was the only thing they had to drink.

"I'm going to see if I can get the door open," Darren said and headed up the staircase.

The door was made of wood and there was a sliding contraption at head height. The hatch was the size of an A4 piece of paper and when Darren tried to slide it open it wouldn't budge.

"It looks like it's locked from the other side," he told the girls. "Same as the door. There's no locking mechanism so it must be bolted and padlocked. We're trapped."

He was about to go back down when a noise made him stop dead. A cough was followed by the sound of shuffling on the other side of the door. The hatch opened and something was shoved through the gap. The plastic bag landed on the top stair next to Darren's feet. The hatch was promptly locked again.

"Let us out, you bitch," Darren yelled. "Let us out. You don't know who you're dealing with."

He could hear the sound of deep breathing. He picked up the bag and inspected the contents. There were packets of crisps and three bottles of mineral water.

"Let us out," Darren said once more. "You're making a big mistake. You're messing with the wrong people. You've locked up Detective Smith's daughter."

The hatch slid open so violently that Darren jumped back. The woman's face filled the gap.

"Let us out now and we won't tell anyone," Darren told her. "You'll regret it if you don't. Lucy is Detective Jason Smith's daughter."

"I know."

The woman's voice sounded different somehow.

"That's precisely the point."

* * *

"What is wrong with this country?"

Smith was staring at the phone in his hand. He'd just finished a call with someone from the HSBC call centre. They'd requested the CCTV footage from the HSBC ATM on Coppergate and the company who operated the security had been very cooperative. The footage would be sent over later that afternoon.

But the details of the transactions on Saturday night wouldn't be available to them until tomorrow. According to the bored-sounding man on the other end of the line, that kid of information needed to be obtained through the proper channels and Smith was informed he wouldn't be able to get anything until tomorrow.

"I thought we lived in a digital world," he said to DC King. "Why can't we get anything done on a Sunday?"

"It's just the way things are, Sarge," she said.

"It's sending out a message to the scumbags, Kerry. Make sure you commit crime on a weekend if you want to get away with it."

"At least we had some luck with the CCTV footage. It's possible we might recognise whoever withdrew the cash."

"I very much doubt that," Smith said. "I need a smoke. Correction – I *really* need a smoke."

He bumped into Whitton by the front desk. She came outside with him.

"I can't get hold of Lucy," she said as they walked.

"Perhaps she hasn't got her phone with her," Smith suggested.

Whitton looked at him as though he'd grown another nose.

"What?" he said.

"When have you ever seen Lucy without her phone?" Whitton said. "A sixteen-year-old without a phone doesn't exist."

"I suppose you're right. She's probably ignoring your calls because she's with Darren bloody Lewis."

"Lucy never ignores my phone calls."

"Why are you so keen to get hold of her?" Smith lit a cigarette.

"I wanted to tell her that we're probably going to be working late. Laura is at Victoria's house, and we haven't taken anything out to eat. I was going to suggest she order a takeaway."

"She'll phone back when she feels like it. The details of the ATM transactions will only be available tomorrow. SAS security – they're the operators of the CCTV cameras at the HSBC ATM, will be sending us the footage shortly, so hopefully we'll know exactly what the person who withdrew the cash looks like, but the bank were about as useful as a one-legged man in an arse kicking competition. Those men are going to die unless we find them soon. I don't think they can last until tomorrow."

Bridge and the DCs King and Moore came outside.

"There you are," Bridge said. "We've had a breakthrough."

"I'm liking the sound of this. Has the CCTV footage come through already?"

"Not yet," Bridge told him. "A bloke in Murton called in about something happening in the house next door. You met him. His name is Jacob Peebles and you spoke to him earlier."

"That's the bloke on Norton Road."

"Number 31," Bridge elaborated. "He called the fire brigade because his cellar was flooding."

"And the fire brigade came out for that?" Whitton asked.

"It's a good job they did," Bridge said. "The water was coming in from the cellar next door."

"There isn't a cellar next door," Smith remembered.

"Apparently, there is," Bridge said. "It's just not in any of the plans at the Deeds office. The fire brigade managed to locate the main water cutoff and when they were busy doing that, they heard someone shouting. They went down to investigate and that's when they found the three men."

"The homeless men have been found?" Smith said. "We need to talk to them."

"That might be a problem. Two of them are dead and the third is in a bad way. He's been taken to hospital, but the doctors are not sounding very optimistic."

CHAPTER FORTY FIVE

Norton Road had probably never seen so much action before. The quiet road in Murton was packed with vehicles of all types. The fire engine was still there. As were three police cars and a host of other cars. Grant Webber's vehicle was one of them. The van belonging to the local TV station was parked as close to number 29 as it could get. Smith's car was still at the garage, so he'd got a lift with Bridge. They slowed down and stopped behind the tape preventing anyone from accessing the house from the road. PC Simon Miller nodded to Smith and raised it enough so Bridge could drive under it. He found a parking spot across the road from the house and he and Smith got out.

"Webber got here quickly," Bridge commented. "I hope Billie is here. I'm thinking of popping the question."

"Where did that come from?" Smith asked.

"I've been thinking about it for a while. I think it's about time I settled down, and Billie is the one."

"That's good to know," Smith said. "But now isn't the time to be thinking about it. You need your mind on the job. We're getting close – I can feel it. We are getting closer."

From the outside it wasn't clear what had happened inside number 29 Norton Road. Early reports suggested a pipe had burst in the cellar and flooded the basement. The water had somehow found its way next door and the cellar belonging to Jacob Peebles had also been affected. The fire department had found three men inside number 29. Two of them were dead, and the other was suffering from severe dehydration. It wasn't yet clear if the men were the three homeless men, but Smith was convinced that they were.

DI Smyth arrived and, after parking his car he made his way over to Smith and Bridge.

"According to the Deeds Office," he said. "The house is registered to a John Simson. Uniform spoke to the neighbour and Jacob Peebles reckons the house has been empty for a couple of months. I've got a door-to-door underway, and Baldwin is busy trying to locate the owner of the house, but so far, he's proving to be a difficult man to track down."

"Do you think he's the man in the mask?" Bridge wondered.

"It's very possible. Where are we with the ATM on Coppergate?"

"We've got the footage back from the security company who operate the cameras," Smith told him. "Harry and Kerry are busy sifting through it, but we'll only be able to get the transaction history from the ATM tomorrow."

"What else do we know?" DI Smyth said.

"We've got two dead men," Smith said. "And a third in critical condition. We don't know what caused the flood in the cellar yet. That third man has to pull through. He's the only person who might be able to tell us who this *Mother* woman is."

A very annoyed looking Grant Webber emerged from number 29. The Head of Forensics looked like a drowned rat. He was drenched. The SOC suit he was wearing was glued to his body and water dripped from him as he walked.

"Is it wet down there?" Smith asked.

"Piss off," Webber said. "The place is knee deep in water."

"What happened?"

"It looks like the man who survived broke the inlet pipe to the radiator. There was a heavy frying pan beneath it."

"Why would he do that?" Bridge asked.

"Because he was parched," Smith said. "The docs said he was severely dehydrated, and he probably did it to get some water."

"I think so too," Webber agreed. "The bath was half full of lukewarm water and the plastic tub from the sink was on the floor in the bathroom section. I'd say it was rather ingenious to think of doing that. Do we know if he's going to make it?"

"It's touch and go," Smith said. "Did you find anything else down there?"

"There was a sodden A4 book on the coffee table. There was nothing written inside but on the front, someone had written *The Cellar Experiment*. That's as far as they got."

"The cellar experiment," Smith repeated. "It's definitely the three homeless men then. Henry, Steve and someone we don't know the identity of. I wonder why they didn't write in the journal."

"It's a pity they didn't. From a forensics perspective that cellar is a fucking nightmare, if you'll pardon my French. Any traces of evidence have been washed clean by boiling water."

Smith took out his cigarettes and lit one. "Did you find an Xbox down there?"

Webber nodded. "Xbox and a television set. It's probably the one they removed from the house in Nunthorpe Road. And Billie found a mobile phone too. It's an iPhone and it was submerged in the radiator water. I very much doubt we'll be able to get anything from it."

"Put it in rice," Bridge suggested. "When I was at university a mate of mine dropped his phone in the toilet. He put it in rice and apparently the rice absorbs the moisture."

"How did he manage to drop a phone into a toilet?" Smith asked.

"Who knows," Bridge said. "Alcohol was involved."

"That makes sense," Smith said.

"I'll give it a go," Webber said.

"We need to hope the surviving victim makes it," Smith said. "And we need to work harder finding the owner of the house."

His phone started to ring. It was Whitton.

"Hey," Smith answered it. "There isn't much to see in Murton."

"I still can't get hold of Lucy," Whitton said. "She isn't answering her phone and I'm getting worried about her."

"She'll be alright. She's probably blasting out music in her room, or in Darren bloody Lewis's room."

"She's not with Darren," Whitton said. "I phoned his mother and she hasn't heard from him either. The same with Jane Banks. All three of them are missing, Jason."

CHAPTER FORTY SIX

"Are there any more crisps?" Darren asked.

"They're finished," Jane informed him. "All we've got left is the bottles of water."

"I'm starving," Lucy said. "And I'm scared. What did she mean back there? What did she mean when she said that's precisely the point? Do you think this has got something to do with my dad?"

"How could it?" It was Jane.

"Jane's right," Darren said. "That psycho woman abducted four Albanians and she's probably the one who took those three homeless blokes, so how could it be linked to Detective Smith?"

"Why did she say that then? When you threatened her and told her I was Smith's daughter she said that was precisely the point. I don't understand."

The hatch in the door at the top of the stairs slid open and Darren was up there in a shot.

"This has gone too far," he said. "Let us out now."

"I'm afraid I can't do that."

The words were accompanied by a whiff of garlic.

"We need some more water," Darren said. "It's too hot down here."

"You do not get to make demands, young man. You're not in charge. You're not important – this is not about you."

"What is it about?"

"I'm going to tell you. Lucy, come closer. This is a good story and you do not want to miss any of it."

Lucy and Jane joined Darren at the top of the staircase.

"I once had a daughter, Lucy," the strange woman began. "Janet was her name, and she was my whole world. I nearly lost her when she was a baby.

You'll soon understand the love only a mother has for a child. You said your child would have been born in August?"

"My child *will* be born in August," Lucy corrected her.

"No it won't. Do you know if it's a boy or a girl?"

"We don't want to know," Darren said. "What the fuck are you going on about? You're going to let us go."

"I don't like the tone of your voice, young man. Janet was a special child. She beat the germs that tried to kill her, and she grew stronger. But then I lost her forever."

"We're sorry to hear that," Lucy said. "But it had nothing to do with us. Why don't you let us go?"

The woman didn't reply to this.

"I got the call early in the morning," she carried on. "It was a Tuesday morning. A typical Tuesday morning like any other. Two cups of tea and the morning paper. Then a phone call made sure that Tuesday mornings would never be normal again. *We're very sorry, Mrs London. We're very sorry to tell you your daughter killed herself late last night. We didn't see it coming. We're so sorry,* they said. They weren't, you know. Janet was one less thing to worry about. There was a full investigation of course."

"Why are you telling us this?" Lucy asked.

"You'll see. The inquiry found nothing untoward. The correctional facility was cleared of all wrongdoing and that was that."

"Janet was in prison?" Darren said.

"She shouldn't have been sent there in the first place."

"What did she do?" Jane asked.

"She was involved in the deaths of a number of police officers."

Lucy felt sick. She could feel her stomach warming up and she could taste bile in her throat. Beads of sweat were forming on her forehead.

"She killed police officers?" Darren said.

"That's correct," the woman confirmed. "But prison wasn't the right decision. My beautiful baby girl needed help, not prison."

Lucy was now starting to feel light-headed. She put her hand on Darren to steady herself.

"Are you alright?" he asked her.

"The truth is dawning," the woman said.

"Lucy," Darren pleaded. "What's wrong? Is it the baby?"

"Your child would have been exceptional. It really would have been extraordinary."

"My child is going to live," Lucy screamed. "You crazy bitch. Open the door."

"Janet was my shining light," the woman said. "And now that light has been extinguished. You cannot imagine the pain in that darkness."

"You're insane," Jane said. "You're stark raving mad."

"She was sent to that place, and that place killed her."

Lucy's heartbeat was speeding up and she wasn't sure how much longer her legs would be able to support her. She let go of Darren and sat down on the carpet at the top of the stairs.

"What's wrong, Lucy?" Darren asked her.

"Her body is reacting to the weight of the truth."

"What's she talking about?" Jane said.

"What's going on?"

Lucy started to cry. She couldn't stop it. Darren crouched down and put his arms around her.

"It's alright. I'm not going to let anything happen to you."

"Her daughter," Lucy managed between sobs. "Janet London. She killed my dad."

"She did not," the woman argued.

"She paid someone to kill him," Lucy carried on.

"Ghosts always come back to haunt you. It's what they're designed to do. Your dad was your whole world, wasn't he?"

"Janet killed him."

"And your *new* dad killed my daughter. As good as. And now he's going to feel the suffering I feel every single day."

"Are you going to kill Detective Smith?" Darren said.

"No, no, no. There would be very little justice in doing that."

Lucy managed to get to her feet. "He'll find us you know. My dad will find us."

"Of that there is little doubt," the woman said. "I'm going to tell him exactly where you are. But not yet. When he finds you, it's going to rip his heart into so many pieces he'll never be whole again."

"Please," Jane said. "Just let us go."

"The Albanians lasted three days. Do you think you can do better than that?"

"Please," Jane said again.

"The woman in the cellar in Richmond Road is already showing signs of giving up. Don't be like Ginnie. I'll be back to check on you in a week. It will be the worst week of DS Smith's life – seven days of pure hell. If I were you, I would drink the water I gave you."

CHAPTER FORTY SEVEN

"How come I didn't know that Lucy likes to come here on Sundays?" Smith asked Whitton as they got out of the car outside Café Noir in Bootham. There was still no word of Lucy, Darren or Jane so Smith had decided to see if he could try and retrace her steps. Darren's mother had promised to keep them informed if Darren got in touch. Jane's parents had promised the same. None of their friends had heard from them and Smith was starting to panic.

"Because you don't listen to a word any of us say," Whitton said. "You never have."

"I'll try and make more of an effort in future," Smith said.

"I'm really worried about her. Something has happened. Nobody has seen any of them since this morning."

"Let see if someone in here can help us figure out where they are."

The same waiter who was working earlier was standing behind the counter. It was almost four and he was cashing up for the day before the coffee shop closed. Smith walked up to him.

"I'm afraid all the machines have been switched off," the waiter said.

"We're not here for coffee," Smith told him. "I was in here earlier with a colleague and another man."

"I remember you."

"Can you remember the three teenagers who came in just before I left?"

"Of course. They're regulars."

"They've gone missing," Whitton said. "We're trying to find them."

"I haven't seen them since they left."

"What time was this?" Smith said.

"About an hour after you did. They left with the old couple."

Smith was suddenly wide awake.

"What did this couple look like?"

"She was short and stocky," the waiter said. "And he was pretty short too. He was wearing one of those face masks."

"Fuck," Smith said. "Excuse me. Do you know where they went?"

"I couldn't tell you. I just remember them leaving with the old man and woman."

"Why would they leave with a couple they didn't know?" Whitton wondered.

"They were chatting before they left the shop. It was quiet in here and I could hear bits of the conversation. It sounded like the woman wanted some help with her computer or something."

"Darren does IT work for people," Whitton said.

Smith looked around the shop. He checked out all four corners of the room.

"Do you have CCTV in here?"

The waiter laughed. "It's a coffee shop, not a bank. Why would we need cameras?"

"Fair enough. What time did the couple arrive?"

"Just after you left. What's going on?"

"We don't know," Whitton said. "Thanks for your time."

* * *

"She's been taken, hasn't she?"

Smith rubbed his eyes. A cup of coffee had been left to go cold on the table in front of him.

"We still don't know that," Whitton said.

"Come on, Erica," Smith said. "Nobody has heard from Lucy, Darren or Jane for hours. It's the same man and woman who the witnesses described. Those bastards have got Lucy."

The CCTV footage of the ATM on Coppergate showed that a man wearing a face mask withdrew some cash from the machine at 8.49 on Saturday night. The footage wasn't great and it was difficult to make out much but his height and build were consistent with the witness accounts. Smith hadn't paid the footage much attention. As far as he was concerned, they had the exact time of the transaction, and the identity of the man would be on the bank records. They would know for certain who withdrew the cash, but that would only be possible tomorrow.

Bridge came in the canteen with DC Moore.

"We've got good news and bad news," he told Smith and Whitton.

"Let's hear the good news first," Smith decided.

"We've got an ID for the man found alive in the cellar in Murton. His name is Marcus Green."

"What's the bad news?" Whitton asked.

"That's as much as he could tell us before he died. His organs just couldn't function anymore. He'd gone without water for far too long."

"Do we know who the other two are?" Smith said.

Bridge shook his head. "We're busy working on it. It's likely it's Henry and Steve. It has to be them. How are you doing?"

"Not great," Smith admitted. "The man who works at the coffee shop Lucy went to earlier told us the three kids were seen leaving with a man and a woman. They matched the description of the couple seen talking to Henry Banks."

"Was the man sure?"

"It's them, Bridge. The bloke was wearing a face mask, and the waiter described a short, stocky woman with brown hair. It's them. Lucy has been taken by the people responsible for the deaths of seven people this week alone. Another woman is still missing, as is our daughter and her two friends. Have there been any other developments?"

"The owner of the house with the flooded cellar," Bridge said. "John Simson. He's dead. Died six months ago and the house is still registered in his name.

Kerry and Harry are trying to track down his relatives."

"The man who lives next door told us there had been nobody living at number 29 for a couple of months. You said Mr Simson has been dead for six?"

"He passed away in a nursing home. He was only there three weeks, and it obviously didn't agree with him."

"Who was looking after the house in his absence?" Whitton asked.

"We don't know yet," Bridge said. "All we know is the house was still registered in his name."

"I wonder why the cellar wasn't on any of the plans," Smith said.

"That's something we'll have to ask the council," Bridge said. "There might be a perfectly reasonable explanation. What's the plan of action?"

"I'm going to find my daughter," Smith said. "I have no fucking idea how I'm going to do that, but I'm going to find her. But first I need a smoke."

CHAPTER FORTY EIGHT

"You lied to me."

Maggie Pratt sipped her tea and winced. It was far too hot, and it tasted bitter. More milk and sugar was needed.

"I didn't lie to you," her friend said. "I just didn't tell you the whole truth. There's a big difference."

"This was supposed to be a social experiment to ascertain how long we as a species could tolerate the extreme conditions the Covid19 restrictions are going to bring. When the virus spreads measures need to be put into place, and we were supposed to provide some answers."

"And that's exactly what we've been doing. The Albanians proved that human beings are extremely resilient. The homeless men were a bit of a disappointment."

"You're lying to me again," Maggie said. "This has always been about you and your revenge. It was never about the virus – this has been about you and your obsession over retribution for what happened after your daughter's own social experiment. That one failed unless you've forgotten."

The other woman had a sudden urge to reach over and throttle her friend of thirty years. She didn't – it wasn't necessary. Maggie Pratt would be dead very soon anyway.

"How long have we known each other?" Maggie asked.

"Thirty years. Thirty good years."

"And we may still have thirty more. We need to start work on the main cellar. The one that might ensure that we survive this thing."

Maggie yawned and finished the tea in her cup.

Her friend smiled and placed a hand over Maggie's. "You're right – I lied to you. I couldn't give a damn about the virus. It can do its worst for all I care."

"What have we been doing this for?"

"Misdirection."

"I'm not following you," Maggie said.

"That's probably because your mind is starting to fog. How was the tea?"

Maggie looked at the cup. "What have you done?"

"Don't worry, your suffering won't be as bad as the others. I suggest you go up to bed."

"What have you done, Heidi?"

"Rest now. It'll all soon be over."

* * *

"Are you going to tell me what the hell is happening here?" Jane Banks was sitting next to Lucy on the sofa in the cellar.

"Don't you remember," Darren said. "Lucy's dad was killed by that bloke in the car park of the Hog's Head."

"He was supposed to be meeting Smith," Lucy took over. "My dad had some information about the Ghosts case, but he was attacked before he could tell Smith anything."

The *Ghosts* investigation was one everybody would remember. The series of police murders was big news at the time. Police officers were being murdered as part of a twisted experiment to demonstrate that the men and women in York Police would prioritise the killings of their own over anything else. A team of university students were carrying out the murders using highly advanced misdirection. The talented amateur magicians were getting away with it and if it hadn't been for the dying words of Dr Nigel Brown Smith was convinced the case would never have been solved. Lucy's biological father's final words were crucial in bringing the investigation to its conclusion.

"And it's looking like the psycho woman's daughter was one of the killers," Darren said. "Madness must run in the family."

"But it's not Lucy's fault her daughter killed herself," Jane pointed out.

"No," Lucy said. "She thinks it's Smith's fault. That bitch blames Smith even though he didn't make her kill herself. She's delusional."

"What are we going to do?" Darren said.

"Wait for my dad to find us."

"What if he doesn't?" Jane said.

"You don't know my dad. He'll find us."

"Doesn't it feel weird calling him that?" Jane said. "You've only been with them for such a short time, and you call them mum and dad like it's the most natural thing in the world."

"It feels right," Lucy said. "My real dad will always be my dad, but Jason and Erica were there from the beginning. They were with me at the hospital when the doctor told me about my dad. I didn't have anywhere to go, and I asked if I could stay with them. Jason said yes without even thinking about it, and when it got to the stage where I'd either have to go and live with a foster family or be adopted by them, he didn't think twice about adopting me. He has his moments but he's a really good dad. He's got a kind heart."

"I obviously haven't been around to see it," Darren said.

"That's because he thinks you're an idiot," Jane said. "And you can't blame him."

"I'm not an idiot."

"You're not too clever either," Jane said. "You have a lot to learn about birth control."

Lucy rubbed her belly. "When we get out of here, I'm going to do everything I can to keep this little thing safe."

"Do you think we will get out of here?" Jane said. "That woman scares the living shit out of me."

"We'll get out of here," Lucy insisted. "My dad is going to find us and we're going to get out of this cellar."

"I don't feel well," Jane said. "I'm dizzy."

"Take deep breaths," Darren told her. "It's probably because of the heat down here."

"I'm feeling a bit weird too," Lucy said. "I feel really faint – like I could fall asleep any minute."

"Maybe that's not such a bad idea," Darren said. "Get some rest and recharge the batteries a bit. Who knows how long it'll be before your dad finds us."

Lucy was now finding it hard to keep her eyes open. Jane's eyelids were also starting to droop. The girls made themselves comfortable on the sofa and soon both were fast asleep. Darren Lewis lasted another five minutes before he followed suit.

CHAPTER FORTY NINE

It was starting to get dark and Smith was feeling more anxious than he'd ever felt in his life. His adopted daughter was out there somewhere, and he had no idea where she was. Lucy, Darren and Jane were probably locked in a cellar somewhere in a city with a population of around two-hundred thousand. She could be anywhere. Seven men had perished in cellars in Scarcroft and Murton and they were yet to make any connection between the properties. Who knew how many other houses the man and woman had access to?

There was a knock on the door of Smith's office and Baldwin came inside. "Sorry to bother you, Sarge," she said. "But I might have found a way to gain access to the ATM records sooner than tomorrow."

"I'm not going to ask how you did that," Smith said.

"It's nothing dodgy. I have a contact who knows a guy who works in the fraud department of HSBC. He has the authority to pull up the records of all the transactions carried out."

"Are you being serious?"

"I am, Sarge. I've set the ball rolling. We know the precise time of the withdrawal and we have an idea of the amount, so we should have the name of the account holder within the hour."

"You're wasted working for York Police," Smith said. "You know that don't you?"

"I happen to love my job. I can't imagine doing anything else."

"And this is all above board?"

"Would you care if it wasn't, Sarge?" Baldwin asked.

"You've got me there."

"I'll let you know as soon as I know anything."

Smith thanked her, and his phone started to ring. The screen told him it was a number not in his contacts.

"Smith," he answered it.

"Do you want the good news or the bad news?" a man asked.

"I'm not in the mood for practical jokes right now," Smith said. "Who is this?"

"Do you want me to fix your car or not?"

Smith realised it must be the mechanic at the garage. He'd forgotten all about his Ford Sierra.

"Sorry," he said. "Give me the good news."

"We can fix the problem."

"Then as far as I'm concerned, there is no bad news. Fix it then."

"But it's going to cost you a bit. The whole starter motor is fried. The brushes, commutator, armature shaft and solenoid are all beyond repair and you're going to need a completely new starter. We can get one by Wednesday and have it fitted by next weekend. It'll be six-hundred ex vat."

"Go ahead," Smith said even though the mechanic may as well have been speaking Chinese.

He really had no idea what he'd just said.

"I'll need a deposit to order the parts."

"WhatsApp me an invoice on this number," Smith said. "I'll pay it immediately."

"Will do, sir."

Smith left the office and went outside for a smoke. He wondered if maybe it was time to buy another car. His contemplation lasted precisely two seconds. He wasn't quite ready to part with the old Ford Sierra just yet. His thoughts turned to Lucy, and he hoped she was OK. It was a blessing that she was with Darren and Jane. She wouldn't have to endure whatever was happening to her alone. Darren could be a bit annoying at times, but

Smith knew deep down his intentions were genuine. He really did seem to care for Lucy and he wouldn't let anything bad happen to her. Jane Banks was also a tough cookie, and she was fiercely loyal. Smith decided that they would be OK for a while.

Baldwin came out to find him and the grin on her face told Smith she was the bearer of good news.

"You've got a name for me, haven't you?" he said.

"Two hundred pounds was withdrawn from the ATM at 8:49 on Saturday night," Baldwin said. "The CCTV showed a man withdrawing the money, but the account holder is a woman."

"Perhaps he used his friend's cash card," Smith suggested.

"The account holder is someone we've spoken to, Sarge."

"I'm listening."

* * *

When Smith went inside the living room of number 10 Nunthorpe Road he thought Maggie Pratt was asleep. The team had rushed straight to Scarcroft as soon as Smith informed DI Smyth they had the identity of the holder of the account the cash was withdrawn from on Saturday night, and they'd gone in mob-handed. The front door wasn't locked and Smith had gone inside the house without even giving it a second thought.

"She's dead."

DI Smyth was standing over the woman on the sofa. He checked her pulse again just to be sure.

"She's definitely dead."

"What the fuck is going on here?" Smith said.

Maggie looked very peaceful in death. Her eyes were closed and she was sitting up on the three-seater. An empty teacup stood on the table in front of her. A large white cat was sitting on the single seater opposite. The cat's eyes were staring, unblinking at its dead owner.

"She doesn't match the description of the woman," DI Smyth pointed out.
Maggie was fairly slim, and her hair was black.

"No," Smith agreed. "She doesn't. But it was her account the cash was
withdrawn from on Saturday night."

"Perhaps her card was stolen," DI Smyth said.

"Sir," Bridge called from the kitchen. "You need to come and take a look
at this."

Smith and DI Smyth left Maggie Pratt alone with her cat and walked down
the hallway towards the kitchen. Bridge was standing next to one of the
cupboards. He was wearing a pair of gloves and he was holding something in
his hand.

"It's a surgical mask," Smith said.

"She was wearing one when me and Whitton spoke to her earlier in the
week," Bridge told him. "But she most certainly wasn't wearing this."

He held it up and everything suddenly became clear to Smith. In Bridge's
hand was a fake grey beard.

CHAPTER FIFTY

"It was two women all along," DI Smyth told the rest of the team. "We were looking for a man and a woman, but we were wrong. Maggie Pratt was wearing a disguise the whole time. She wore a surgical mask over a fake grey beard."

Grant Webber was still busy at the house in Nunthorpe Road. It was possible he would find something in Maggie Pratt's house that would lead them to the other woman, and ultimately to the cellar where Smith was convinced Lucy was being held. Maggie's cause of death was unclear and Smith wasn't particularly interested in that anyway. He needed answers about Maggie's accomplice, and he needed those answers now.

"What else do we know about Mrs Pratt?" he asked.

"Not much," DI Smyth said.

"Me and Whitton spoke to her straight after the Albanians were discovered," Bridge said. "She didn't sound any warning bells."

"It makes sense when you think about it," Smith said. "She lives next door, so she won't have had any problem getting into the house without arousing suspicion. We need to find out who she was working with. Who are her friends? The face mask suggests she's germ-phobic and that makes me think these so-called experiments are linked to the Covid thing, but we still have no idea who her accomplice is. Do we know anything else about the family of the man who owned the house in Murton?"

"We haven't been able to find out much," DC Moore told him. "It's Sunday and people are a bit reluctant to help on a Sunday."

"I don't give a fuck what day it is, Harry. Our daughter is locked in a cellar somewhere out there. *She* doesn't care if it's Sunday. I want to know who has access to the house in Murton and I want to know that now."

"Calm down," DI Smyth said. "You need to calm down and stay focused. We've found one of them, and it's only a matter of time before we find the other woman."

"We didn't even consider that she could be using a disguise," Whitton said.

"Why would we?" Smith said. "These two are good. We've been looking for a man and a woman all along and they've succeeded in sending us on a wild goose chase. Maggie Pratt had opportunity in Scarcroft, but what are her ties to the house in Murton? We find a link between any of her friends and that house, we find the other killer. We need to put all our efforts into the house on Norton Road."

"Smith's right," DI Smyth agreed. "It's late but I don't care. We'll carry on through the night if we have to."

"I'm cool with that," Bridge seconded.

"Me too," DC King joined in. She turned to Smith and Whitton. "We will find Lucy. I promise you we will find her."

The clock on the screen of Smith's laptop told him it was almost nine. Darkness had arrived hours ago, and it would remain for a good few hours yet. Smith thought of Lucy and her friends locked up in a cellar somewhere and he shivered. The thought made him feel sick to the stomach. It also made him wonder why the three friends were taken. The Albanians and the three homeless men were easy prey, as was the woman who was persuaded to go with the couple under the ruse of a housesitting job, but where did Lucy, Darren and Jane fit into the plan? Surely the abductors would know they would be missed straight away. They were upping the stakes with this one, and the risks were considerably higher. Smith couldn't figure out why they'd deviated. The MO was the same, but the motivation still eluded the experienced detective.

After reading the same sentence on the screen for the third time and failing to register what he was reading Smith admitted defeat. He couldn't concentrate. The files from the Deeds Office weren't giving him anything useful. The house on Norton Road was registered to a man by the name of John Simson. John had passed away in a nursing home six months ago, but the house was still registered in his name. There was nothing in the records to suggest that the property had since changed hands. There was no mention of a relative or friend inheriting the house and no records of the place being rented out.

Smith needed a break. He needed some fresh air to clear his head. He left the office and headed down the corridor. He was halfway to the front desk when someone shouted.

"Sarge. I've found something."

It was DC King. She and DC Moore were with Bridge in his office. Smith went straight in.

"What is it, Kerry?" he said.

"You need to look at this," DC King turned her laptop around, so it was facing Smith.

He took a step closer. "What am I looking at?"

"John Simson has a daughter, Sarge," DC King said. "Heidi. She's fifty-six years old and she was the one responsible for putting her father in the nursing home."

"Do you think she did that so she'd have access to his house?" Bridge wondered.

"That's not important," Smith said. "Do we know where this Heidi Simson is now?"

"Heidi London, Sarge," DC King corrected. "She married and her name is now Heidi London."

"The previous owner of the house in Scarcroft." Smith had cottoned on.

"The very same. And there's more. When we spoke to her, she said she'd bought the place in Nunthorpe Road because of the cellar. She said she had two teenage boys, and they could use the cellar to chill out. She lied. She doesn't have two sons – she has one daughter. Or at least she did have a daughter."

"What happened to her?" Smith said.

"She's dead. She committed suicide three months ago in Lingdale Correctional Facility."

"That's the women's prison in Leeds."

"Her name was Janet London, Sarge."

Smith suddenly felt very cold. His skin was tingling.

"Ghosts," he said in a voice no louder than a whisper.

"She was involved in the police murders," Whitton remembered too.

"And she was Heidi London's daughter. I think you've found your motive, Sarge."

"This wasn't about some twisted experiment," Smith said. "The Albanians and the homeless people were a smokescreen. Misdirection at its best. Lucy was the target all along, wasn't she?"

"I think she was, Sarge," DC King said.

"And I know where she is," Smith added.

CHAPTER FIFTY ONE

"Smith," DI Smyth said. "You and Whitton are to stay right where you are."

"You know I can't do that, boss," Smith said,

"This isn't up for debate," DI Smyth told him. "Consider it a direct order. Both of you are too personally involved in this."

"I need to see this through to the end."

"Not going to happen. We have a good idea where Lucy is, and we are more than capable of carrying this out without you."

Smith took out his warrant card and put it on the table.

"What is this?"

"My badge," Smith said. "I am not staying behind to wait for a phone call. I'm going to finish this. Take the ID and try and stop me."

DI Smyth sighed. "You'll be the death of me. Put that thing back in your pocket and stop behaving like a spoilt brat."

"You're not going to stop me," Smith insisted.

"We'll discuss this later. We don't believe Heidi London is armed, but I want backup in place just in case. A team has been briefed and they're on their way to the property in Clifton. With any luck we'll have the advantage of surprise on our side. I don't think Mrs London will be anticipating this."

"Don't underestimate her, boss," Smith said. "Everything she's done so far has been carefully planned. She's orchestrated every step, and she will have made allowances for every possible eventuality. Her daughter was a master of misdirection and it's looking like she learned everything she knew from her mother. Let's get moving."

Smith drove with Bridge. DI Smyth was close behind, and DC King and DC Moore brought up the rear. Two police cars were also in the convoy. Heidi London was one woman, but DI Smyth wasn't taking any chances. It was possible she'd be prepared, and her actions thus far had proven she wasn't a woman to underestimate. The DI had devised a quick plan of action. The house in Clifton was situated in the middle of a row of semi-detached properties. The gardens at the back faced Hill Street and there would be uniformed officers in place there. Two more officers would stand sentry at the side of the house. Smith had insisted he be the first one inside the house and DI Smyth didn't argue. It would have been pointless to do so.

Bridge parked his Toyota about fifty metres away from number 24 Baker Street. The rest of the team arrived shortly afterwards. Smith closed his eyes and took a moment to compose himself.

"Are you alright?" Bridge asked.

Smith nodded. "I'm going to get my daughter back."

"Do you think she's got any tricks up her sleeve?"

"We won't know until we go in."

"It's possible she might not even be home," Bridge said. "There's no way she would know we'd be onto her so soon."

"Don't assume anything," Smith said.

"You've been inside the house," Bridge said. "You and Kerry spoke to her yesterday. Did you notice if there was a cellar?"

"I wasn't looking for one. We stayed in the living room."

"And you didn't suspect anything?" Bridge asked.

"Heidi London wasn't a suspect," Smith reminded him. "I didn't get any weird vibes from her, if that's what you're asking."

"Murderers come in all shapes and sizes. We should know that by now."

"Let's go and see what we're dealing with, shall we?"

Smith got out of the car and headed straight for number 24 without saying anything further. He needed some answers, and he needed them now. As he walked up the path to the front door the first thing he registered was the house was in darkness. There were no lights switched on inside. The streetlight outside was the only source of light close to the house. Smith heard footsteps behind him and when he turned around, he saw it was DI Smyth. The DI shook his head to indicate that Smith wasn't to go in just yet.

Smith paid him no attention. He placed his hand on the door handle and pushed open the door. He stood for a moment and listened carefully. The house was silent. He stepped inside with DI Smyth close behind him.

The lights suddenly came on and Smith was blinded for a second. He heard the sound of a door slamming close by.

"You check the living room," DI Smyth whispered. "I'll see if I can find a cellar."

"I don't think there is one," Smith said.

"I'll check anyway."

"Don't bother."

The voice sounded like it was coming from the kitchen at the end of the hallway.

"You're not going to find them."

Heidi London appeared in the doorway. She was holding something in her hand. Smith took a step back. Then he realised what she was holding – it was a tablet.

"I think it's time you and I had a little chat, don't you?" she said to Smith.

"I think that's a very good idea," Smith agreed.

"I won't offer you anything to drink if that's OK with you."

"And I wouldn't drink anything you offered me anyway," Smith told her.

"Shall we talk somewhere more comfortable?"

She walked past him and DI Smyth and went into the living room. The two detectives followed her in.

"Take a seat," Heidi said. "We have a lot to discuss."

Smith and DI Smyth both sat on the three-seater. Heidi sat opposite them. She glanced at the screen of the tablet and put it down on the coffee table.

"This was hardly what could be described as a covert operation, Smith," she said. "I saw you coming a mile away. All of you. I suppose the element of surprise is something you've yet to learn."

"There's a lot I've yet to learn, Heidi," Smith told her. "I want to know why you did this. I want to understand what drove you to kill all those people."

"Simple misdirection. Maggie planted the seed in my head when she became obsessed with the virus. There is a lot of fear out there – most of it harboured by the people with the power, but simple people are lapping it up. Maggie was one of those people. The idea of the experiment came to me in a flash of inspiration. Maggie and I are women with considerable means, and I spotted an opportunity too good to pass up on."

"You murdered seven innocent men," DI Smyth said. "You locked them up and let them die in the most horrible way."

"In a game of chess it is often necessary to sacrifice the pawns."

She glanced at the tablet again.

"What are you looking at?" Smith asked her.

"I'll show you in a minute," Heidi said.

"Why Lucy?" Smith came out with it. "Why did you take Lucy and her friends?"

"You're going to feel what I felt. You're going to suffer unbearable pain."

"I'm not responsible for your daughter's suicide, Heidi. You cannot possibly think that was my fault."

"Of course it was your fault. You were the one who sent her to that place."

"Your daughter murdered five police officers," DI Smyth reminded her. "She was responsible for the death of Lucy's biological father. She deserved to go to jail. The only person to blame for her choosing to end her own life is Janet. Nobody else can take that blame."

"Aren't you going to ask where they are?" Heidi said.

"No," Smith replied. "Was Maggie Pratt one of your pawns too? Was she someone who could be sacrificed when she was no longer needed?"

"She'd fulfilled her part of the plan. Poor Maggie. She was a good friend, but she was delusional. She truly believed we were doing this for the greater good. She really thought we were using those homeless men in an experiment for the benefit of mankind."

"You're sick, Heidi," Smith said.

"And it's all over," DI Smyth said. "You can't magic your way out of this one. No amount of misdirection is going to get you out of this."

"You're still forgetting the ace I'm holding. I know where Smith's daughter is, and you don't. I won't tell you that until it's too late."

"You'll die in prison, Heidi," Smith told her. "You'll probably be sent to the same place where Janet died, so I suppose there's some comfort in that."

"I'm going to make you suffer irreparable damage, Detective Smith. You will never recover from this. Do you want to see what's on my tablet now? Look at it if you don't believe what I'm telling you."

Smith gave DI Smyth a subtle nod and the DI left the room.

"What's going on?" Heidi asked.

"We're going to arrest you," Smith informed her. "But we're not taking any chances. You can go quietly, or you can make it hard for yourself, but you will be restrained. Show me what you're so keen for me to watch."

Heidi swiped the screen of the tablet and an image appeared on it. She tapped play and Smith saw movement in the bottom corner. Heidi zoomed in on the figure on the bottom rung of the staircase. It was Lucy.

"She looks scared," Heidi said. "Her friends are there too."

Smith nodded. "She looks OK to me."

"She won't look like that in a few days' time."

"No," Smith agreed. "She'll be back home by then."

They carried on watching. There was no sound on the footage, but it didn't matter. They didn't need audio to understand what happened next. "What on God's earth…"

Heidi London's mouth opened so wide Smith could see a full set of false teeth. Her eyes were glued to the screen.

"I hope you're recording this," he said.

There was a flurry of activity on the screen now. The rapid movement of the players involved in the action made it unclear what was actually happening. Darren Lewis's face appeared for a second or two and then Smith saw Whitton. She was standing in front of PC Black and PC Miller. Baldwin appeared for a split second too. Then an image appeared that Smith would remember for the rest of his life. Jane Banks and Darren Lewis had been led up the stairs and only Whitton and Lucy remained in the shot. Smith wasn't sure how long the embrace lasted, but later when he watched the footage again, he would realise his wife and daughter had hugged for precisely twenty-six seconds.

CHAPTER FIFTY TWO

"How are you doing?"

Smith was sitting next to the bed Lucy was on. She was sitting up and she was holding Whitton's hand. The three friends had been taken from the cottage in Barmston by ambulance to York City Hospital. Darren and Jane had been checked over and discharged but the doctors wanted to keep Lucy in overnight just to be on the safe side. Lucy and the baby were going to be fine but until they knew what the three teenagers were drugged with, they didn't want to take any chances.

Smith knew straight away where the friends had been taken. He recalled Heidi mentioning the cottage by the sea and when he checked he realised Heidi had been telling the truth about it. The two-bedroom holiday home had a cellar and that was enough for Smith. Whitton and the PCs Black and Miller arrived in Barmston the same time Smith and the team got to Heidi's house in Clifton. DI Smyth had wondered why Smith had chosen not to go with them, and Smith told him it wasn't necessary. Whitton and the uniforms were more than capable of getting the teenagers out of the cellar and he was determined to get his motive straight out of the horse's mouth.

Heidi London hadn't spoken a word since she was arrested but she did say something when she realised what was happening on the screen of the tablet.

How?

Smith had replied with one word of his own.

Misdirection.

It was all over. Lucy, Darren and Jane were safe, and Heidi London was heading where she belonged. She would live out the rest of her days in the prison where her daughter did the same.

"I feel fine," Lucy said. "I feel OK and they're making me stay in hospital overnight."

"Welcome to my world," Smith said.

"Did they find the other woman?"

"She's right here in this hospital," Whitton told her.

"That was a very selfless thing you did," Smith added.

In the ambulance on the way to York Lucy's main concern had been the woman who was taken on Saturday night. She remembered Heidi mentioning something about Ginnie being held in a house in Richmond Road and that was enough for the team to locate the property. Ginnie was severely dehydrated but she was going to be OK.

"You probably saved her life," Whitton said. "And we're so proud of you."

"I'm so sorry it happened," Smith said.

"It's not your fault," Lucy said. "It wasn't as bad as it could have been. Darren and Jane were there and we stuck together. Darren was amazing. He's never going to let anything happen to me, Dad. He even made me drink more water than he did. We didn't know the water had been drugged. It's probably why I passed out before he did."

Lucy had told them they'd woken up in a different place. All three friends had fallen asleep in the cellar in Clifton and woken somewhere else. Smith assumed they'd been transported to Barmston while they were unconscious. Heidi London would probably tell them the whole story someday, but right now Smith wasn't interested in hearing it. Lucy was safe and that's all that mattered.

A young doctor came in and smiled at Lucy.

"She needs to get some rest," he said to Smith and Whitton.

"We'll come and see you in the morning," Whitton told Lucy.

Smith stood up, leaned over and kissed Lucy on the head.

"Something doesn't feel right," he said.

"What are you talking about?" Whitton said.

"The investigation is over. We've cracked the case, and I don't have so much as a scratch on me. It's not right."

Whitton laughed. "Don't tempt fate, Jason."

Lucy laughed too. "You're weird."

"And you're stuck with us," Smith said.

"She really does need to get some rest," the doctor said.

"We're going," Smith told him.

"We'll see you in the morning," Whitton said. "Sleep well."

Darren Lewis and Jane Banks were standing in the corridor outside the room when Smith and Whitton came out.

"How is she?" Darren asked.

"She'll be fine," Smith said. "She just needs to rest."

"I would have never let anything happen to her," Darren said. "To Lucy or the baby."

"I know you wouldn't," Smith said. "I'll see you later."

Darren held out his hand for Smith to shake. Smith looked at it then he looked at the expression on the teenage boy's face. Darren looked utterly exhausted. He looked like he could sleep for a week. Smith took a step forward and wrapped his arms around the teenage boy. Darren stiffened and then Smith felt his shoulders relax. He hugged Smith back. Smith broke the embrace first.

"See you soon, Darren."

"What was that all about?" Whitton asked Smith in the car park.

"Darren isn't so bad," Smith told her. "I think he's right for Lucy."

Whitton looked at him with deep concern in her eyes.

"Are you alright? Are you sure you didn't get hit on the head because you sound like you might have concussion."

"There's nothing wrong with my head," Smith said. "Darren is starting to grow on me."

"Are there any other flashes of inspiration you'd like to share with me? Any more sudden insights?"

"No," Smith said. "Oh, the boss is gay by the way."

"And you've only just figured that out?"

Smith stopped dead. "You knew?"

Whitton kissed him on the cheek. "For an ace detective, your powers of observation are severely lacking at times."

Smith kissed her back. "I'll see if I can work on that."

THE END

Printed in Great Britain
by Amazon

36337884R00136